CRATERTOWN

Hal Barwood

life on Mars
a criminological adventure

Cratertown

ISBN 978-1-7354222-6-8

This is a work of fiction. Mars is real enough, and human ambitions regarding it are also real. But currently the red planet is not inhabited, except possibly by very small and cryptic life forms. Accordingly, all the characters and incidents depicted herein are products of the author's imagination. No resemblance to any real institution, government agency, enterprise, or person is intended.

Acknowledgments . . .

Many thanks to the adventurous readers willing to explore unfinished versions of this tale: The Barwoods, Barbara, Jonathan, Tobias, Curt Blanchard, Robert Dalva, and Beverly Graves.

Thanks to Google, Wikipedia, and the rest of the World Wide Web for enabling the author's virtual exploration of this book's exotic terrain.

About the Author . . .

Hal Barwood is a veteran writer and designer. You can find out all about him right here . . .

www.finitearts.com

for

NASA, ESA, Roscosmos, CNSA,
JAXA, ISRO, UAESA

maybe they'll get us there

Table of Contents

Inhabitants of The Ark

Joseph Ford (Joe)
  . . . immigrant maintenance engineer

Hesperia Dale (Hes)
  . . . native-born farmer, designer, and part-time teacher

Eridania Rooney, MD (Dana)
  . . . visitor; habitat doctor working off her medical school debt

Ismenius Pomerance
  . . . native-born Counselor to the Like Minded

Nilosyrtis Hoberman (Nilo), Lycus Salazar (Liko),
Trivium Quinn (Triv)
  . . . native-born Active Deacons of the Like Minded

Hadley Timmerman
  . . . astronaut who founded the habitat

Thuvia Lofgren (Thoo)
  . . . native-born journalist

Zoran Boskovoy
  . . . visitor; astronomer, exobiologist, and part-time journalist

Erebus Imowelo (Ed)
  . . . native-born customs agent and maintenance supervisor

Bradley Mayfield (Buster)
  . . . immigrant farmer

Town Manager (Tammy)
  . . . avatar of the township's main computer

Motro
  . . . an industrial robot

If we say we have no sin,
we deceive ourselves,
and the truth is not in us.

— 1 John 1:8

STEP ONE

1

W AKE UP, please, Passenger Ford. Time to wake up."

Joe Ford's sleep-encrusted eyelids, clamped tightly shut, twitched. His fog-shrouded mind registered a bell chiming softly. A neutral female voice was quietly calling him from a tinny loudspeaker: "Wake up, please, Passenger Ford. This is your wake-up call."

He wasn't ready. His eyelids seemed welded together. His head was spinning. He ran his tongue along the roof of his mouth. It scraped like a wool sock on cement.

Now the voice broke into song — *"Wake up, wake up, you sleepyhead; wake up, get out of bed . . ."*

A vivid dream was drifting away as consciousness returned. It was a good one. He tried to chase it — a long walk through a cool forest, following a trail as it switched back and forth across a limestone mountain face. Tall conifers sharp against blue sky. Puffy clouds promising afternoon showers. Where was he? Somewhere in the Sacramento mountains of southern New Mexico, maybe? What was he doing there?

The bell became an annoying buzz. The female voice took on urgency — "Wake up, Passenger Ford. Show me you are awake."

Suddenly three jet fighters slammed through his reverie. Fireballs engulfed the trees. He found himself in a dank stucco jail cell. The iron bars clanged shut.

"Aahhh!"

He jerked upright, straining against his sleeping bag. He felt woozy, hopelessly confused. Where am I now? Not in jail, praise the Lord, but where? It took him a moment of careful attention to pry his eyes open, carefully peeling the goo from his lashes. He was in a tiny cubicle. He squinted at a sign posted on the door:

ACCOMMODATION MODULE 15
WELCOME ABOARD INTERPLANETARY CYCLER-03
GOD SPEED YOU

Now he remembered. No wonder he was dizzy. He was weightless, for Heaven's sake, cruising through interplanetary space, slowly coming out of anesthesia. An intravenous tube emerged from his right forearm and disappeared into the ceiling overhead. For some unknown length of time it must have been pumping him full of stimulants, nudging him back toward consciousness. He yanked it out, rebelling against the chemicals. He kicked out of the sleeping bag, floated across the narrow space and touched a keypad. The female voice seemed much relieved:

"There you are, Passenger Ford. Good morning. Press the keys, please, as they light up."

The keypad began to wink in a random pattern. His fingers tracked the lights from key to key. The female voice conceded approval: "Very good. You're alert. Report to the flight deck, please."

"Is this an emergency?" he growled.

"No, Passenger Ford. We have arrived."

"Then I have to take a leak."

In one corner of his compartment stood a vacuum toilet. He got himself into position and drained a long trip's worth of urine.

Above the toilet was a small jet sink, and above that a mirror. He snapped on the tiny overhead light and took a look at himself. Light brown eyes over a straight nose. Flecks of grey in his shaggy hair. Whiskers sprouting all over his angular jaw. Thirty-five years old looking fifty, he thought. God, he was tired. He squirted a blob of yellow lather from a small tube, rubbed it across his face, and wiped it off with a paper towelette. His beard came with it. That's better. At least now he didn't look like Rip Van Winkle.

Clad in a baby blue paper jump suit, he braced himself with one hand and rotated the door latch through a ninety degree arc. The anchor pins withdrew and the door angled inward, cracking the seal. A gust of stale air whistled in around him. He shivered and floated through.

The Cycler, he thought. A space ship. From inside it looked just like a large silo. Or a warehouse. Two dozen or so cargo containers were strapped to the expanded metal mesh that constituted the ship's decking. His tiny cabin appeared to be the only one prepared for human habitation.

A motorized cable, painted red and white like a barber pole, stretched through the central axis of the ship in a long loop, pulling flexible tow lines in opposite directions. Groggily, he grabbed the handhold as one of them glided by. It yanked him toward a door at the far end emblazoned:

FLIGHT DECK

Inside, he strapped himself into one of twenty-four acceleration chairs behind the command station.

"Where is everybody? Where's the pilot?" he demanded.

"Right here, Passenger Ford," cooed the female voice.

Of course, he realized, there was no pilot. This was the ship talking.

"You mean, that's it, I'm the only actual human being?"

"On this trip. Don't you remember?"

"Christ. How long have I been out?"

" Sixty-three days. Are you hungry?"

A tray hummed into position from beneath his seat, steaming with gluey foodstuffs. He grimaced.

"You call this a meal?"

"We're outward bound, Passenger Ford. Acclimatization policy."

"I'm cold."

"Look for a blanket in the panel under your seat."

Grumpily, he threw it over himself. He felt like a sick kid.

"I am rotating the ship. You should have a fine view in another thirty degrees."

For the first time, he realized that the black wedge-shaped portals above the command station were unshuttered. He was already looking outside, but lights on the flight deck, dim as they were, still made it impossible to see anything in the inky darkness of space. After a few seconds, though, rays from what seemed to be a powerful searchlight splashed across the heavy polycarbonate window and into the flight deck.

In another moment the source of the light moved into his field of view: a dazzling pink-white sphere, twice as close as the moon and eight times as bright. Joe Ford's eyes teared up. He held up a hand to ward off the frightening glare.

"Ouch."

"Don't be alarmed. Your eyes will adapt. Find dark glasses in the arm rest if you need them. Docking at Phobos Station in four hours and ten minutes."

He found the glasses, put them on. Now he could make out some details. There, a blazing white crescent: the South Polar Cap. Above it in the far East, a pink oval a thousand miles across: Hellas Basin. Slashing across the middle was the great scar of Valles Marineris, a complex of trenches four miles deep and longer than the distance from New York to Los Angeles. On the horizon to the northwest was a dark blip trailing a long white cloud. It could only be Olympus Mons, tallest mountain in the solar system, poking its lofty head over the rim of this fantastic world. The rest of the visible surface was pock-marked and barren, utterly alien.

Thus did Joe Ford get his first good look at The Red Planet Mars. "Why," he wondered aloud, "would anyone in his right mind volunteer to live on this godforsaken slag heap?"

2

HESPERIA DALE pulled a mask of polymer netting over her face, tucked her sleeves into kevlar gloves, and adjusted the flow rate on her smoke generator. Satisfied, she made her way along a tubelike passageway to an airlock showing red warning lights. She threw a switch, and the lights turned green. She tugged at the door. It opened, and she passed through. In three strides she reached a second door and another set of warning lights. She threw another switch, waited until the lights turned green, and pulled hard. Reluctantly it came unstuck. Hot moist air greeted her, pungent with the odor of ammonia.

She took a step across the threshold, and there she was, down on the Farm again. Thirty-six hectares of greenery, divided among dozens of gigantic greenhouses, stretched away in front of her for seven hundred meters. The arched polymer roof, once clear and sparkling, had long since become cloudy with age and exposure, but the light was still more than sufficient for rapid cultivation. It was her favorite place in The Ark — the name colonists bestowed on Human Habitat One, shortly after it was established by the Planetary Settlement Agency.

"You lied to me, babe. You said, no more queens." It was a cheerful accusation. Dale turned toward the voice. Emerging from a jungle of banana plants was leathery Buster Mayfield, the only full-time farmer on the planet.

"Where are they now?"

"Guava patch." He grinned. "You won't believe it."

Mayfield led the way through the bananas, past row after row of soybeans and through an archway. As they started into the second greenhouse, Dale could hear an angry buzz over the soft purr of the air conditioning.

"There. Where in hell did they come from?" Mayfield pointed to a small pear tree just beyond a thicket of guavas. Hanging in the branches was a writhing mass of living tissue the size of a football. *Apis mellifera* — honey bees.

"You call that a swarm? There can't be ten thousand animals." Dale was annoyed.

"Sorry, Hesper. We gotta make the ID."

"Do you know what day this is?" She looked at her watch.

"Work comes first, girl."

"Yes. Work comes first. I know." She frowned. Mayfield was an Immigrant, and he held to the old ways.

"Get your vac ready." Dale turned her smoke generator on the wriggling bugs, enveloping them in a thick grey cloud. Mayfield's vacuum cleaner sucked the now docile insects into a clear plastic container. She delicately plucked those the nozzle couldn't reach with her fingertips and dumped them in on top of the rest.

"Help me sort them."

At the inner end of the Farm was the beekeeper's station. Mayfield inverted his container over the sorting box and opened the inlet. Dale flipped a switch and bent over the clear acrylic top as one bee after another was dropped singly down the sorting chute and onto a rotating platform. After observing a thousand or so workers centrifuged off into a new hive without finding the queen, Dale began to feel desperate. She looked at her watch again. "Come on, come on. Where is she!?"

Finally a larger bee spun off the platform at a looser angle, right into a waiting flask. Dale held it up for close inspection. It was, in fact, a queen. Printed onto the thorax of the buzzing insect was a tiny strip of bar code, robotically generated by a hive monitor. Dale flicked a laser pencil past the markings and read the result off a display screen at her elbow.

"Queen 17, Hive 3, plantation 9."

Mayfield shouldered his vacuum cleaner. "They shouldn't be hatching queens. We better get out there."

Dale, exasperated, pushed the flask into his hands. "You do it. They're de-orbiting the ferry at 13:30. And I'm not dressed."

Mayfield stared at her, jaw working silently. "That's the trouble with you youngsters. You got duties. You got obligations. You got to fulfill 'em."

Dale said nothing. She pulled the netting from her head and removed her gloves.

Mayfield shook his head. "I'll take care of the bees. I don't mind. It's not you, girl, it's the whole thing. Getting worn down. People got secrets now. They're making deals. Oh yes, I've seen it. Deacons, too."

"Hey. Save my soul tomorrow, okay? After you log a new tag on number 17 there." She leaned forward, gave him a quick kiss on the cheek, and bolted out of the airlock.

3

ON EAST CENTRAL BOULEVARD, Dale hurried along with the crowd, clutching a small bouquet of white onion flowers and biting her lip to keep from cursing her fellow citizens. The thoroughfare, widest in the Township, was barely eight meters from wall to wall. And it was jammed with people hurrying, like herself, to catch a glimpse of the ferry as it flew in from Phobos. Pushing and shoving were never good manners here, and Dale abruptly slowed as she realized that she was bound to miss the big event.

Ismenius Pomerance, an older man with curly dark hair, dark eyes, and a sharp nose, fell into step beside her. "You're late. You'll never get into the dome now."

Dale regarded him coolly. "Hello, Counselor. I'll call my privilege. Someone will give way."

"You don't want to do that. You'll look like a fool. Come on, I've saved you a place on the bus." Pomerance stopped. He gestured toward a narrow alleyway intersecting the main street.

"Really?" This was privilege indeed.

"I thought you might want to meet the passenger."

"Guess I better, huh?" She smiled a tight smile.

Pomerance smiled back and led the way into the alley, turning right through a heavy steel door, moving east along another corridor, stepping through a large airlock and out into a cold and noisy garage. There a large number of all-terrain vehicles were parked, jammed together within the narrow confines. Many were undergoing maintenance and repairs. The chattering of air tools and the ringing of metal on metal split the air. Some of the machines were large, some were small, but all were distinguished by their outsize spoked wheels, taller than a man, with aluminum slats set crosswise, like a picket fence, in place of tires. The largest of all was ten meters long, with a row of windows down each side, and six enormous wheels. Workmen were busy covering it with red and white bunting. "Welcome to the Independent Republic of Mars," read a sign across the nose.

Pomerance guided Dale to the boarding ramp and followed her inside. Cargo handlers, paramedics, a reporter, and a video crew were already aboard. There was a round of warm applause as Dale settled into her seat. She acknowledged it with a wave, blushing to the roots of her reddish blonde hair. Pomerance nodded to the driver. The power pack kicked in and electric motors began to hum. The bus rolled slowly forward onto a barely visible track imprinted on a wide sandy plain. They were outside.

On the horizon the sky was pale pink, the result of rusty dust suspended in the lower atmosphere; but overhead, where the air was too thin to scatter any light, the sky was almost black. Out of it the sun glowered down, fierce but faint.

Flight Operations Center, their destination, was five kilometers northeast of the colony, and a hundred meters lower. In laying out their air and space port, habitat engineers had taken advantage of the enormous flat bottom of an ancient network of riverbeds, known since the early days of planetary exploration as Tiu Valles. The ferry, when it landed, would touch down where the waters of Mars had once flowed magisterially north into Chryse Planitia, the sea.

Dale rarely ventured outside, so she was both excited and apprehensive as the big wheels of the bus rolled slowly over the small volcanic blocks and crater ejecta in their not-very-well-worn path.

"Here it is!" shouted Pomerance, pointing out the window.

Dale and the rest of the passengers craned their necks upward. High in the west the ferry, a graceful white spaceplane with wide sweptback wings, flashed over them at several hundred miles an hour. There was a faint double thump as the sonic boom drummed the thin Martian air, and then it was gone again, disappearing into an easterly haze.

The bus descended the gentle slope into the center of the ancient riverbed. Half a klik away Dale could see the white domes and half-cylindrical hangars of Flight Ops. As they arrived, the ferry circled around on its final approach, traveling much slower now. She watched its absurdly large flaps come down, watched dust swirl as superheated air blasted downward from its engines, balancing the spaceplane against the weak Martian gravity. Then it was on the ground, taxiing toward the hangar.

The bus arrived first, slipping through the freight airlock at one end of the aluminum structure. Apart from the Farm, this was the largest enclosed space in the Township, a fact dictated by the need to accommodate the ferry's sixty-five meter wingspan.

The bus came to a halt in the customs bay, separated from the hangar itself by clear polycarbonate windows. There was no airlock for the huge spaceplane. Instead, one entire wall of the outer hangar was wide open. Through it Dale could see the ferry lumbering toward them, wings drooping. Dale's fellow passengers hurriedly gathered up their gear and hopped off the bus, intent on recording the spaceplane's arrival on video. Dale herself started to follow, but stopped short as Pomerance's hand gripped her arm.

"Wait a moment, Sister. I need to talk to you."

Dale shrugged his hand away. "What about? What do you mean?"

"How well do you know this man, Joseph Ford?"

"Are you kidding? I don't know him at all."

"And yet you're willing to marry him?"

"I've said so, and attested such before the gathering, haven't I?"

"Yes. Of course. You have a public spirit we all admire." He looked at her closely, gauging her. "Tell me, you've exchanged calls?"

"Yes."

"Does he seem fitting to you?"

"He's okay. He's an Immigrant."

"Will he make you happy, do you think?"

She bristled. "How should I know? You've got nerve, Ismenius, butting into my life."

"Your life doesn't concern me. Go your way with God's blessing. It's the life of The Ark I'm thinking about. You're a part of it. A vital citizen."

Dale looked at him, at his dark unblinking eyes. "Does this sermon have a point?"

"Joseph Ford will, I sincerely hope, prove to be a loving husband and valuable addition to the IRM. But you should know that, whatever else he may be, he is undoubtedly an Earthly spy."

"What?"

"A North American Fed. Recruited during the Mexican Operation."

"Why are you doing this to me?"

"Hesperia, please. I just want you to remember who your friends are. I want you to remember who he is."

"Inform on him, you mean. For the good of our good old Republic." Her mouth twisted ironically.

"Yes. And why not? Possibly this fellow is here to do us harm. But his loyalties may change. We're a small group, struggling against long odds. He may sympathize. We may win him over. You'll be his wife; a lot of it's up to you . . ." Pomerance let the thought hang.

Dale's face was reddening. "You're telling me, don't let us down, show him a good time."

"That's not what I meant."

"I'll handle my own life, thank you just the same. Leave me alone." She brushed past him and stalked off the bus into the already pressurized customs bay, just in time to see the hangar doors close behind the ferry.

Pomerance came up behind her. He started to apologize, but his voice was drowned out in the roar of a howling wind as huge pumps strained to pressurize the hangar and make its air breathable.

Under the ferry, technicians were inspecting the jet nozzles, checking for tritium leakage. Radioactivity was never a problem with ground-based fusors, but the tremendous power and light construction of flight reactors always made everyone a little nervous.

Finally, one of the men signaled a happy pad, and Dale found herself walking through the customs bay airlock and into the hangar proper. Her head was spinning. Pomerance had made it impossible to concentrate on the moment. She felt like a robot: one foot in front of the other, marching to someone else's drum. Why was she doing this? Why had she volunteered?

As she stepped into the hangar she caught the acrid tang of Martian dust. Like a dose of smelling salts, it woke her up. Her heart skipped a beat as the ferry's hatch cracked open with a report like an air hammer. She stopped walking. Too late now, she thought, he's here.

Technicians wheeled a stairway into place. There was a long moment of silence, broken only by the ferry's airframe, still creaking as it cooled. Then a booted foot appeared in the hatchway, followed by another. Hands reached down and deposited a large duffle on the stairway platform. Cargo handlers rushed up the stairs to carry it and several others that followed into the customs bay. Dale still couldn't see the figure clearly. But finally the man from Earth started down the stairs, bobbing uncertainly in the Martian gravity, and Dale had her chance to size him up. She was shocked. He was short and swarthy by Martian standards. As he approached the welcoming committee, turning this way and that to take in his new surroundings, he seemed stooped and feral. Heavenly Father, she thought, he looks like an ape.

Joe Ford was thoroughly disoriented. He had spent two days on Phobos while the Planetary Cycler's cargo was transferred to the ferry. He had bounced all over the station trying to move around in the feeble gravity of Mars' inner moon. The station medic had drawn a lot of blood, checking to be absolutely sure he was free of disease. He had watched the pale ochre surface of Mars spin underneath five and a half times, and with every revolution the monotony of the colors, the innumerable craters, the lack of water, and the lack of any evidence of the hand of man, had thrown him into a deeper and deeper gloom. Now he was bobbing up and down on the surface, trying to teach his muscles how to behave in a real gravity field after more than two months of weightlessness.

Waiting for him in the hangar were a dozen people. They didn't seem particularly glad to see him. He wasn't sure if that bothered him or not; he hardly knew what to expect. As he wobbled forward his eyes fastened on a tall thin woman with strawberry blonde hair. She was holding a small bouquet of wilted onion flowers, and she was staring at him. Why is she so thin, he wondered. She looks like a stick. Is she ill? Then, with a jolt, he recognized her: this was the woman he had come to Mars to marry. Good God; she didn't look at all like the videos.

"Joseph Ford, meet Hesperia Dale." Pomerance stepped forward to make the introduction. Video cameras moved in to capture the moment.

"Hello," he said.

"Welcome to The Ark," she replied and handed him the onion flowers. The onlookers applauded.

He fumbled in his shoulder bag and produced a sealed plastic box. Under the clear cover, small plants were growing in mica-filled potting soil. "Here. This is for you."

"Siberian strawberries! How did you know?" Dale was surprised and pleased. Her face colored. The onlookers chuckled.

"Someone named Mayfield. Soil guy, right? He sent me a note. He said you'd like them."

"Oh yes."

Ford felt awkward. He dug into his bag again and pulled out a silvery disk, the size of a coin. "I also brought this. There's two hundred and fifty-six feature films on there; five seasons of *Geo Specials;* all the episodes from last year's *Doctor Grogan at Law* — that was a big hit — all the novels recommended by *Readers Review* for the past decade, plus three hundred and sixty-five days of *The New York Times*, and good shots of the new island off Hawaii. You know, it's still erupting."

The onlookers fell silent. Ford could see he had breached some rule of etiquette, but he couldn't imagine what it was. Dale hesitantly took the disk, mindful of critical eyes upon her. "I accept your gift in the spirit in which it is offered, and hereby declare a donation to the Town Library," she said, with great formality. She handed the disk off to Pomerance as the onlookers nodded approval.

Ford winced. "Oh yeah. Got it, good idea."

With the ease of a practiced politician, Pomerance turned toward the video cameras and cleared his throat. "Now, Joseph Ford, it gives me great pleasure to say, in my capacity as Counselor to the citizens of The Ark — welcome to your new home! This is a great day. Let us rejoice, that another free man has cast his fate with the New World. Here is a new friend and a new pair of hands to help us shape our future and mold our dreams into the stuff of life."

"Amen," said Ford.

▼

In the customs bay the cargo handlers opened all his bags, pawed through his possessions, and inspected every item.

"What's this?" asked the black middle-aged customs agent, holding up a shiny tool.

"A variable wrench."

"We have plenty of wrenches. You know how much it cost to haul this thing all the way from Earth?" The man was clearly offended.

"Call me sentimental. I've turned a lot of bolts with that wrench."

The agent lifted a small device with dangling wires and a tiny display screen. "This?"

"Multiprobe."

"Ours aren't good enough?"

"Frankly, I doubt it."

The agent nodded ironically. "You might be right there. And this?" He poked at a tray filled with plastic wafers smaller than his fingernails.

"My library."

"Open the bottle, please."

Ford cranked the top off a plastic vial. Pale green pills spilled into his hand. The agent's eyebrows shot up.

"Tranquilizers. I've got a prescription," Ford explained.

"You know, the medics won't issue norvalin or any other chemical depressant here. We don't use them."

"So I was told."

"With any luck Mars will calm you down before you run out, and you won't miss them."

"That's what I'm hoping." Ford carefully repackaged the medicine.

The agent handed Ford a magnetic sign with the digits *5-0-3* stuck on it. "Hold this up and smile at me." He aimed a camera and flashed Ford's picture.

"Passport?"

Ford gave him his North American passport. The agent drilled it with a laser:

CANCELLED

Then he fed a sheet of plastic into his computer terminal. He guided Ford's thumb onto a sensing pad and pressed a key. A moment later out came a small plastic rectangle emblazoned with the newcomer's name, picture and thumb print.

"That's you: Joseph Ford. Valued Citizen number five hundred and three. Congratulations, you're official." He reached out and shook Ford's hand. "I'm Ed Imowelo, customs king."

"Remember — this little handheld is your ID, your money, your phone, your keys. Hang onto it."

Ford inspected the thing. It wasn't much thicker than a credit card. Quaint technology twenty years out of date.

"We'll return your wrench and your — whatchacallit? — multiprobe and library after we take a closer look."

▼

The bus toiled slowly out of the wide riverbed and up the slope toward the Township. Joe Ford and Hesperia Dale sat side by side, both feeling uncomfortable facing a reporter who was aiming a video camera at them.

"I'm Thuvia Lofgren, ATV," burbled the journalist, an eager young woman barely out of adolescence. "Now that you're here, Brother Ford, it must be very exciting. Could you describe your first impressions of Mars for us?"

Ford looked ahead. Spread out across a wide shelf of umber land enclosed within the vast expanse of Klickitat Crater was a hodgepodge collection of long low buildings and domes, altogether spanning more than a kilometer — the better part of a mile. Except for half a dozen impressively large radio antennas, a power station, three water tanks and the many greenhouses, the place seemed completely undistinguished.

"That's The Ark?" he asked.

"That's it. We've lived here all our lives so we're used to it. It must be quite a sight to you."

Ford thought it looked a lot like one of the big poultry farms on the outskirts of Albuquerque. Or, perhaps more kindly, one of the many business parks filled with featureless tilt-up warehouses on the west bank of the Rio Grande.

Lofgren stuck a microphone under his chin.

PODCAST HOST:
Hello, friends. Thuvia, *The Real Maid of Mars* here, coming to you from Ark Bus Zero Three. With me is our new arrival from Earth, Joseph Ford. We're rolling back from the ferry landing to his future life in our habitat.

FORD:
Call me Joe.

PODCAST HOST:

All right — Joe it is. So, hey, Joe, you're a long way from Earth now. Welcome to Cratertown.

FORD:

Cratertown? Is that what you call it?

PODCAST HOST:

Sometimes. Local term. It's affectionate.

FORD:

Sounds kind of low-rent for such a heroic achievement, don't you think?

PODCAST HOST:

The Ark has its foibles, like anywhere. Like a lot of places back on Earth, I guess, huh? We're at peace with them.

FORD:

Sure.

PODCAST HOST:

Soon you will be too.

FORD:

Counting on it.

PODCAST HOST:

And you're here to marry this beautiful woman by your side, is that right? It's all arranged?

FORD:

That's the plan.

PODCAST HOST:

Ever been married?

FORD:

Nope. This is a first for me.

PODCAST HOST:

Well, we wish you both the best. Hesperia is one of our leading citizens. A terrific catch, if I do say so.

FORD:

(He touches Dale's arm.) Couldn't agree more.

PODCAST HOST:

Marriage means joining our little band of true believers. Mars is unforgiving, and life in The Ark is a full-time adventure. You're a brave man.

FORD:

(Smiles.) Bravery? What's that? I fell for her picture. The videos we sent each other.

PODCAST HOST:

That is *so romantic.* Give me, give my listeners, here and back on Big Blue, your reaction, first impressions, what you see out there on the crater floor, what you think of it all.

FORD:

Well, the habitat, it's a lot bigger than I thought. A small city, really. It's beautiful. Very, um, striking, I would say. White buildings on red dirt. They really stand out. It looks like — like my new home.

PODCAST HOST:

Thank you, Joe. There you have it, people. We're not standing still here, we're growing. Today it's Joe Ford. Tomorrow — maybe one of you will show up next.

4

THE NEWCOMER was sitting on a spindly aluminum chair in the awkwardly tiny cubicle that served as Ismenius Pomerance's executive offices, sipping a cup of bitter green tea.

On Earth, a room this size would be somebody's closet, he thought. He ran his thumb around the rim of his cup, feeling the crack there. He shifted his weight. The chair creaked underneath him. Everything was old and worn.

He wondered about the dark-haired man sitting across the dented pull-down desk, studying his dossier. Born here, of course. Probably one of the first, forty years ago or more. Was he a pious soul? A dull bureaucrat? A heroic pioneer? The recent immigrant didn't know what to think.

Pomerance looked up. *"Joseph Elias Ford.* Both parents and a sister. All three deceased."

"Yes. We were living in New Mexico when the Dividers made their move. It happened during the Civil War. First week."

"I'm terribly sorry. I thought I knew all about you."

"That's okay. It was years ago."

Pomerance's brow clouded with sudden worry. "I believe we explained Dale's recent bereavement, did we not? In one of my messages? You have heard the news?"

"Her husband died. You told me. She told me. Don't worry, I know what I'm getting into."

Pomerance looked relieved. "That's good. All eyes are open. Now that you've met her, are you still prepared to make her your life's partner?"

"Is there a problem? Does she want to back out?"

"On the contrary."

"Well, okay. I'm her man."

"All right, then. It's settled." He glanced back at the dossier. "One last thing. Your family wasn't Like Minded."

Ford shook his head. "Catholics. Not very good ones."

"Were you confirmed?"

"You're recording this, am I right? You're wondering why I converted."

Pomerance acknowledged the reproach with a smile and a shrug. "It's my job to wonder. I'm the Counselor."

"Well look, I can't tell you the reason, because I don't know myself. Foxhole religion, I guess. At the start, anyway."

Pomerance wasn't satisfied with Ford's explanation. "Like the British Puritans five hundred years ago, who settled a wild and unpromising land in North America, we're settling a New World, with new opportunities for the betterment of humanity.

"But Mars is harsh, terribly harsh, harsh beyond belief, and like our forebears, without a profound faith in ourselves, our future, our God, we wouldn't last another day. Do you yourself have such faith?"

"Here I am, Counselor. I traveled two hundred million kilometers to find out the answer."

Pomerance nodded. "Very good. Well said."

All at once the desk lamp began to buzz and flicker like a stroboscope. Pomerance twiddled the dimmer, to no avail. "This happens every now and then," he apologized. "Probably a power surge."

"Allow me." Ford struck the fixture a sharp blow with the heel of his hand. The buzzing stopped. The light steadied.

"Well. Is that what they teach maintenance engineers?" Pomerance suspiciously tried the dimmer again.

Ford smiled. "First lesson, on the first day."

The door opened, and a hefty young man slipped inside. With all three of them in the tiny compartment there was barely room to breathe.

"Joseph Ford, Lycus Salazar. Lycus is one of our Active Deacons."

"Welcome to The Ark, Brother." Salazar grasped Ford's hand and pumped it with enthusiasm. "Action in harmony," he intoned.

"Harmony in thought," Ford replied, careful to use the proper words.

"And thought in action," said Salazar, completing the litany. "I can't tell you how it helps our work, to have the example of your commitment." With a gesture of respect, he handed the Earthman a roll of paper neatly tied with red ribbon.

Ford untied the ribbon and unrolled the paper. It was a baggy white cassock.

"What's this?"

Pomerance grinned. "Your wedding gown."

5

ACTIVE DEACON Salazar marched along Southwest
Lateral with long easy strides. Joe Ford bobbed clumsily at his
heels, cassock flapping. He was still trying to get the hang of
gravity only thirty-eight per cent as strong as Earth's. Luckily
there was nobody around to collide with him.

"Where is everybody?" he wanted to know.

"Working, probably. Don't worry, you won't be alone here
very often."

Ford didn't doubt it. He was in a sour mood, bothered by the
cramped style of life revealed in the low ceilings of the corridor,
in the fire-fighting stations and emergency pressure suits he saw at
every intersection, in the endlessly repeated pre-fab modules that
told him the entire settlement had once been inside a freighter
from Earth, and above all in the pungent human odors that
assaulted his nose in waves as they walked.

"Air conditioning problem?" he asked.

"I beg your pardon?" Salazar seemed oblivious. Ford decided
not to pursue it.

Southwest Lateral ended at a pair of doors. Salazar came to a
halt in front of them. "Here we are."

"How do I look?" Ford adjusted the ridiculous cassock.

"Like a man who understands the solemnity of the occasion.
Ready, Brother?"

Ford popped a tranquilizer into his mouth. "As I'll ever be."

Salazar pushed open the doors and led the newcomer through
the airlock into Central Park.

At Ford's appearance, a wave of applause echoed off the walls
and polymer roof, thoroughly embarrassing the man from Earth.

Many of the citizens of the Township were there, more than a hundred people all told, standing on a hectare of grass around a surprisingly large pond. At one end a real willow tree hung its branches low over the water. Standing nearby with Ismenius Pomerance close at hand was Hesperia Dale, clad, like Ford, in a white paper cassock. She had woven pink guava blossoms into her hair.

As he came near, he began to revise his appraisal of her physical appearance. Compared to her fellow Martians, she didn't seem particularly thin or tall. Although she must have been cooped up in Cratertown all her life, he thought she had an outdoorsy quality. Her lips parted in a gracious smile of encouragement as he took his place at her side. Close up, her hazel eyes sparkled.

"Who gives this woman's hand in marriage?" Pomerance's voice carried across the pond from the far side, where the Counselor was guiding a motorized wheelchair toward the wedding couple.

"The New World," roared an old codger in a wheelchair.

"And who this man?" asked Pomerance, positioning the wheelchair in front of the little group.

"The Old World," said Ford. He studied the wheelchair's occupant. He was very old, spare and leathery, with an aura of wispy white hair floating above his head. Thick optronic glasses covered his eyes. Oversize hearing aids were stuck in both ears. Every few moments he inhaled from a portable oxygen bottle. Ford guessed without being told that this must be Hadley "Tug" Timmerman, legendary astronaut, explorer, and Founder of Mars' Human Habitat One, also known as The Ark, the Township, and with a hint of disparagement, Cratertown.

"Welcome to our great enterprise, Brother Ford," boomed the old man. Welcome to the Independent Republic of Mars!" His voice, young and resonant, surprised Ford. Then he spotted a synthesizer under the wheelchair.

The old man's hand twitched on a joystick, and he spun himself around to face the gathering.

"Valued citizens, listen to me," he thundered. "Our beloved Red Planet has circled the sun almost forty times since we took responsibility for the future of the human race and declared our new civilization. In that span, while our world has prospered at its slow and stately pace, the Earth has endured endless years of turmoil. Disaster after disaster. War and starvation. High crimes and low misery."

Timmerman paused in his oration for a slug of oxygen.

"Some believe that mankind is cursed, forever doomed to repeat his sins, generation after generation unto extinction. But we do not share this grim pessimism. And so we've brought our hopes to a new home in a new territory. We've lost the Garden, so we've steered our Ark a little east of Eden, into the land of Nod. Inhospitable to human flesh perhaps, but fast friend to Like-Minded spirits."

Ford listened to the round tones blasting out of the shriveled figure with amazement and grudging respect. There was power and authority in the voice that didn't come from any synthesizer.

"From time to time the light shines on a hitherto darkened soul, and we add that soul to our number. Thus do we enlarge and establish our blessings, while the society we left behind plunges deeper into corruption."

The old man paused again, panting. Then, summoning new strength, he abruptly stood up out of the wheelchair and raised his arms to the audience.

"Now I ask: shall we today, in great joy, bind Joe Ford into our midst through marriage to our dear Sister, Hesperia Dale?"

After the opening solemnities, Ford was surprised to hear a lusty cheer from the gathering: "Yes! Yes! Yes!"

Timmerman smiled a lopsided smile. "Well, then, Brother Ford: wilt thou have this woman to thy wedded wife, forsaking all others, till death do you part?"

"I will," said Ford, glancing at Dale.

"He will! He will! He will!" chanted the crowd.

"And thou, Hesperia, wilt thou have this man to thy husband, and cleave unto him only, till death do you part?"

"I will," said she, staring straight ahead.

"She will! She will!" echoed the crowd, in great good humor.

"Do thou, Joseph, promise to love and keep her, for better or for worse, till the end of your days?"

"I do."

"He does! He does! Hooray!" yelled the crowd.

"And do you, Hesperia, promise to love and keep him, in sickness and in health, till the end of your days?"

Dale's eyes were misting over. She swallowed and nodded. "I do."

"She does! She does!" The crowd clapped and cheered.

"Is there a ring?" Timmerman wanted to know.

"There is." Ford wrestled a fine gold band from his little finger and slipped it into place on Dale's left hand. She echoed his pledge with a gaudily anodized titanium ring of her own design.

"Done! In my capacity as a responsible citizen of Cratertown, I hereby pronounce you man and wife. Lord, bless this union — let it rain!"

Somewhere a pump started thrumming. Heads tilted toward the roof as a column of water gargled through the network of pipes hanging just below the rafters. Following a series of chattering bangs a few drops fell on the upturned faces. Then, with a tired wheeze, the pump failed, and the rain stopped.

The old man's strength vanished as suddenly as it had appeared, and he dropped back into the wheelchair for a long drag on his oxygen supply.

A heavy silence descended on the gathering. Ford and Dale stood awkwardly facing each other.

Pomerance stepped forward to rescue the moment. "I think we're wet enough. You may kiss the bride, Joe."

"Yes! Go! Kiss the bride! Kiss the bride!" demanded the crowd.

They both knew the ritual, as traditional on Mars as on Earth, but neither made a move. Ford tried a smile that came out as a grimace. "I'm game if you are."

Dale's eyes flashed defiantly, but she inclined her head toward him. Ford took her lightly by the shoulders, and the two strangers kissed.

The citizens of Mars went wild.

▼

In the Main Street Food Hall the revelers danced for hours. An autonomous synthesizer provided the tunes, deliberately stupid but infectious polkas, waltzes, and salsa hip-swingers. Nearly every woman on Mars claimed a turn with the newcomer, and Ford discovered some of the benefits of weighing less than he was used to. Dale danced a long slow waltz with Pomerance, spinning gracefully around the mall, which is what Main Street really was.

The Barsoom Bakery shop provided a cake with pink and brown frosting. They ate it all. The water company supplied a sparkling drink that tasted like sour beer without the alcohol. They consumed it by the keg.

Ford met somebody — who was it? — and learned all about the famous salt deposits on the floor of Chryse Planitia.

He discussed South American grains with Buster Mayfield.

He told Thuvia Lofgren and Township Television all about his life on Earth.

PODCAST HOST:
What was it like growing up?

FORD:
Youngest kid in the family. School at New Mexico State in Las Cruces, then the War and the Army.

PODCAST HOST:
You saw combat? Bet that was fun.

FORD:
What do you think? Americans killing and maiming each other. A dirty job.

PODCAST HOST:
I'm so sorry. I didn't mean to be flippant.

FORD:
That's okay. Now I'm here.

PODCAST HOST:
Yes! You are! Congratulations on the big move and your beautiful new wife!

He hardly noticed that he and Dale had said not a word to each other.

After a sumptuous soybean dinner catered by the McMars refectory (which Ford found strange but palatable) by popular demand he and Dale did a turn on the dance floor. They were both stiff and self-conscious, but the onlookers never noticed.

When the music stopped, the laughing merrymakers lifted the newlyweds onto their shoulders and carried them away, marching through the hallways and laterals to the East Residence District, where they deposited the pair at Dale's front door.

"Get inside now," admonished Buster Mayfield, with a devilish grin. "It's time for married folks to be home in bed."

Dale showed her handheld ID card to the decoder, and the door sprang open. As she started to step inside a collective gasp went up from the crowd.

"What? What is it?" she demanded.

"Joe, save this woman from herself," said Mayfield.

So Ford picked her up — his Earth muscles made her seem as light as a feather — and carried her across the threshold. The door slid shut, but the boisterous throng made no move to disperse. Instead, they began a rhythmic clapping. After a minute of this, Dale, looking very red in the face, re-opened the door.

"Thank you for seeing us home. Now good night to you. Leave us in peace."

In the constricted society of The Ark, a direct request for privacy was treated with respect, and accordingly, with many a gripe and grumble, the celebrants drifted away.

▼

"Here we are," Dale said, with a little shrug.

"Here we are," Ford agreed.

He looked around the apartment. Except for a training period in Antarctica and, briefly, on the Moon, he had never experienced living quarters quite so cramped. There were two narrow rooms: a dining nook which doubled as the kitchen, and a living area which was also the bedroom. A shower and toilet hid themselves in a tiny stall beyond the food heater. The effect was softened,, ever so slightly, by pale blue walls and a large TV screen that slowly cycled through lush views of Earth's forests and telescopic portraits of the outer planets.

"Nice place," he said, lamely attempting to conceal his dismay.

Dale regarded the alien man whose bulk seemed to fill her entire home.

"You know the original name for the colony?"

"I probably should, but I don't."

"*New Hope.* Except in the official Latin nomenclature it comes out *Nova Spes*. No space — get it?"

In the last century railroads had carried plenty of people across North America in accommodations not much bigger than this, Ford reminded himself. They called them *sleeper cars*.

"I don't know," he said. "It looks . . . kind of cozy."

"They do say optimism is the true sign of an Immigrant."

Dale turned a cold eye on Ford's luggage. Three bags! A hundred and fifty liters worth, at least. Where would they put it all? She was irritated that customs had made the delivery without asking her permission.

"Is that all your stuff — I hope?"

Ford nodded.

"Help me get it into storage." She unfolded a bed from the wall, revealing closet space behind. Ford set about unpacking. When Dale had crammed the closet full she unlatched the attic bin in the ceiling and hoisted the rest of Ford's gear up inside. After a tough struggle to squeeze it shut, she sat down on the bed.

"Earth people own too much."

"Bad habits die hard." Ford sat down beside her. He handed over a photocube of the Old World.

"In one of your transmissions you told me your family came from California. I thought maybe you'd like to see what it looks like from orbit."

She turned the clear resin block this way and that, examining the gorgeous globe within. Blue water and spiraling white clouds spoke eloquently of a fertility her own world would never possess. Curving through the center was the western rim of North America.

"Use this." He handed her a magnifying lens.

Under the fresnel ridges she could make out a fine network of lines converging in the middle of the Big Valley. "So that's Fresno.

My father grew up there. It looks hot. It looks hot and miserable and polluted and poisoned."

"I guess it does. Why your folks left?"

She swallowed. "They went back. I stayed."

She thrust the photocube into Ford's hands like a hot potato. "You should donate this to the library. That's where it belongs, where everyone can see it."

"I brought it for you."

She leveled her gaze at him. Who was this stranger, she wondered, this creature from another planet, with his heavy bones and muscles and his old world attitudes? How did I marry him?

"Are you a spy?" she asked.

"Am I what?"

"I was told you're an Old World spy. I'm supposed to watch you."

"What are you talking about? Who told you that?"

"Ismenius. He thinks you're up to something."

"The Counselor? I'm as Like-Minded as he is."

"Well, I won't do it. I don't care what brought you here. Makes no difference to me."

"I'm not a spy."

"Fine. Do whatever you want, and I'll do the same. I won't be used by anyone, not by our esteemed and blessed Counselor, and certainly not by you."

Ford winced at the bitterness in her voice.

"Your husband died when? Six, seven months ago?"

"Yes . . . six."

Ford made an effort to understand what brought Dale to this unhappy moment. "And right away somebody said — this guy Ismenius, probably — forget him already, you're eligible, you owe it to Mars to marry the Earth spy."

"I agreed to marry you of my own free will."

"Why did they let me come, if they think I'm subversive?"

"The Township needs skilled people, you know that. The geologist, Roy Harman — he was their first choice. Then he got sick."

"I know. We trained together. Hepatitis is a disqualifying disease."

"I'm not complaining. He meant nothing to me."

"Look, I'm sorry about your husband. I'm sorry about hepatitis. But I'm not sorry I'm here."

"Mmm."

"And especially not sorry I found you."

"Really? Let's get something straight. You wanted to immigrate, I've agreed to be your sponsor. But that's all. That's what this marriage amounts to."

"Claro." Ford stood up from the bed as if it had suddenly caught fire. "Don't worry — I'll sleep on the floor." He looked around. "Assuming we can find a spot big enough."

"No. That won't work."

"Why not? We're both under a lot of pressure here. I don't mind."

"You don't understand."

"Yes I do. Low gravity, right? I'll be okay."

"Listen, will you please? You can't stay here tonight. You have to leave."

"What?" Ford was stunned.

"I won't have you in my apartment overnight." Ford heard no sympathy in her stone-cold voice. None at all.

"Wait a minute. Where am I supposed to go?"

"I'd suggest Main Street. You can curl up on one of the benches."

"I can't do that. People will see me."

"Probably."

"Are you crazy? We'll be the talk of the Township."

She handed him a pillow and a blanket. "That, Brother Ford, is the whole idea."

6

JOE FORD wandered miserably through the darkened laterals of East Residence District, looking for somewhere, anywhere, to curl up for the night. He imagined the tiny apartments behind the doors he passed, and the people wedged into them like sardines. At least they had beds.

On reaching the airlock leading to East Central Boulevard he stopped. Footsteps and laughter were echoing faintly through the hallway behind him. Oh no. Now what to do? Itching with embarrassment, he looked around for a place to hide. There was none. He decided to face whoever it was and be damned, but just as a small group of people came in sight at a far intersection he ducked into the airlock instead.

That was stupid, he told himself, as he hurried along the passageway. Had they called to him? He wasn't sure. Probably they were just workers coming off the swing shift. Probably they didn't realize who he was, anyway. He hurried on. At least there didn't seem to be anyone else around to bother him. And, he noticed, he was getting a lot better at walking in reduced gravity.

At the next intersection he veered into a northbound lateral and stopped again. There in a parking alcove was a small electric freight truck. Aha!, he thought, a secure bivouac. He climbed into the load space and hunkered down on the floor, listening for sounds of human activity. There was none; just the quiet rush of air through the ventilation ducts overhead. After a moment he began to relax. He wrapped himself in his blanket and waited for sleep to come. What a day.

As his eyes began to droop he heard voices. Two or three people were having a conference ten meters away in the intersection:

"Gotta be him. Who else would be out here?"

"Sorry son of a bitch."

"Okay, you head for the Park, I'll check the laterals."

Footsteps clattered on the floor, moving away. Ford was wide awake again. Pretty soon, they'd be back. Damn. He hopped out of the freight truck and headed north.

He turned west into a connecting corridor, then south, then west again. He was now hopelessly lost.

"Hey — Brother Ford!" They had found him. Three men were standing in the intersection he had just come through, waving cheerfully.

Ford ducked into a narrow alleyway, sprinted its length, and emerged back in East Central Boulevard. Facing him was another airlock. Behind him came quick footfalls and loud halloos. There didn't seem to be much choice. He stepped through the double doors and found himself on Main Street.

Waiting for him there were a dozen citizens. They laughed at the look of consternation on his face and let out a cheer as he stepped into their midst.

"Why Brother Ford, what brings you out on your wedding night?"

"What's the matter, couldn't get it up?"

"Wouldn't give you a chance is more like it, eh?"

"Let's see the blanket! Show us the pillow!"

Ford was mighty annoyed. He dropped the blanket and pillow on the floor and just stared at them. They howled.

"The joke's on me," Ford said.

"That it is, Brother." Someone placed a crown of paper horns on his head. Everyone clapped and hooted.

"Tell us all about her. Tough woman, am I right?"

"Yeah, she's tough." Ford grimaced.

"You argued and pleaded."

"I did indeed." He was starting to get into the spirit of the occasion.

"Heart of stone, right?"

"Heart of stone."

There was another cheer.

"Have a cup of coffee, soldier — long night tonight." Buster Mayfield handed him a cup of steaming liquid and led him to one of the tables in front of the coffee vendor's little shop. Scowling, Ford gulped down the bitter brew.

"You might have warned me," he said.

"What? And spoil all our fun?"

"I guess not."

"Don't be too hard on us. Arranged marriages are pretty common here. It's a way of letting the Township know that whatever happens, happens with a woman's consent, you understand?"

"Where in hell am I supposed to live?"

"Oh, she'll take you back in tomorrow, now she's made her point. Don't you worry none. She's a good woman, and she knows what's what, believe me."

Ed Imowelo, the customs agent, approached the table with a plastic bottle full of brown liquid. He screwed the cap off and, with a mischievous wink, topped up Ford's cup. "A toast to Joe Ford from his new friends." They all lifted their cups and glasses. As Ford took a swig tears sprang into his eyes.

"What's in this stuff?" he wheezed.

Imowelo shook his head. "No one knows. Some say medicinal alcohol, and some say there's a functioning still somewhere in Cratertown."

"I don't know anything about it," said Mayfield. "And now,

gentlemen, I'll be saying good night to you." He stood up and walked away.

"Alcohol's proscribed," Ford said without thinking. It was one of the tenets. He looked at the group of men, suddenly silent. Their faces had the guilty expressions of naughty schoolboys.

"What the hell. Fill me up." He held out his cup, and Imowelo refilled it. He offered a toast: "Here's to The Ark and its valued citizens."

There was a murmur of assent.

"And, if she ever takes me back, to my wife."

This was enough to restore the good mood. Someone produced a keyboard, someone else a drum, and the music started. Imowelo burst into song:

> *It rains in Spain*
> *in the plain I've heard tell,*
> *and it rains in Zambia too.*
> *It rains in England*
> *where the bumbershoots bloom,*
> *and it rains way down in Hell.*
> *But nary a drop does there fall on Mars,*
> *no never a rainbow here.*
> *we've got sunny weather from*
> *May to December*
> *and all the rest of the year.*

A lean unshaven fellow in a dirty pressure suit liner sidled over to where Ford was watching the fun and tipped his glass. "Congratulations, Brother," he said. "Looks like you're on the team."

"Pardon me?"

"A little drink now and then never hurt anyone, right?"

Ford shrugged. "When in Rome."

"Against the rules, of course. But we make exceptions, right?"

"What is it — are you one of Ismenius' Active Deacons?"

"No, I'm a scientist. And part-time journalist. Everyone here juggles their work."

"Well, write me up, I don't care." Ford started to down another jolt of his potent cocktail.

"Tell me, why immigrate? Can't be the allure of that cool goddess, the widow Dale."

Ford sat back, stung by the remark. He tabled his drink.

"Why not?"

"I don't know. Something's funny."

Ford studied the man, his what-the-hell look and manner. "You the Background Man?"

"Zoran Boskovoy, at your service."

Ford felt his skin tighten. "Okay, friend. No idea what you're talking about."

Boskovoy leaned forward. "Roy Harman. An old colleague of mine. He was chosen, then bumped. I doubt he really got hepatitis."

Ford perked up. The guy was speculating about something, but obviously clueless. "It happens. Too bad for him, and my good luck."

"Looks that way."

Ford scowled. "Journalism? Is this conversation turning into an interview? I've had enough, thank you."

7

THE SCIENTIST was getting ready to probe further when he was interrupted by a buxom woman sashaying toward their table with a smile on her lips and a drink in her hand.

"Don't get up, Zoran. I just want to say hello to our newcomer."

She pulled up a chair and sat herself down, sliding wide hips onto the seat and clicking her glass against Ford's as she did so.

"*Salute!*" she said.

"Cheers."

Boskovoy grinned. "May I present Eridania Rooney . . ? She's our local doctor. You know, M.D. Keeps us on our feet . . . most of the time. Very skillful lady."

Ford nodded politely. "Nice to meet you."

"Call me Dana."

"Joe."

"Watch out, Brother Ford. She's not shy."

Ford suppressed an appreciative grin. The woman was certainly attractive . . . and obviously aware of her effect on men.

She arched an eyebrow. "Don't pay any attention to Zoran here. He attempted to climb Mount Dale and failed."

Boskovoy snorted, stood up, and reached out to shake Ford's hand.

"Welcome to Mars, Joe," he said, walking away.

Rooney watched him wander off among the guests.

"Well, that's Zoran. He's got curiosity, he's smart, and he's shrewd, but my God, what a jerk."

Ford cracked a smile. "This is how you speak of your fellow citizens?"

Rooney laughed. "Call it like it is, right?"

Ford registered her knowing eyes, her bronze skin, her compact stature, her familiar tone. "You weren't born here, were you?"

"Earthers — we've got to stick together."

"Thought so. Where you from?"

"Minneapolis, up in Minnesota. You?"

"Albuquerque."

"War zone, I hear."

"Was . . . for a while."

Rooney downed her drink. She leaned forward, placed a hand on Ford's arm. "You're looking for the Background Man?"

Ford froze. "Good God, Where do you people get these ideas?"

She bit her lip and cast a sidelong glance to be sure no one could overhear. Then: "That's me, *comprende?*"

Ford rocked back in his chair. "You sent the messages?"

"Yeah."

"I've read some of your dispatches," Ford said carefully, using the agreed-upon formula.

"Which ones caught your eye?" It was the correct reply.

"I liked the accident report best. Very informative."

A wave of relief swept over the woman's face. "So. They did send an agent. Thank God."

Ford's expression soured. "I like the word *scout* myself."

"When I heard they turned down that guy — what's his name? Harman? — for immigration, I thought things might be shaping up. But I wasn't sure."

"Hepatitis is hard to catch nowadays," Ford acknowledged. "So tell me, what's going on?"

She twirled her empty glass around. "Truth is, I don't know, but there's trouble. You're Like Minded? I mean, really? True believer?"

Ford shrugged.

"Not me. The system they've got here sounds idyllic, but it's not working."

"How so?"

She placed her elbows on the table, lowered her chin into her hands.

"Township records show three deaths by asphyxiation, two during the first years of the colony, and they both occurred when EVA suits malfunctioned. Number three, though, P.L. Scott — he died in the West Side Auxiliary. Sudden decompression."

Ford cocked his head. "Go on, how did it happen?"

"Meteor strike."

"Well, hello boys and girls, that's a big hazard on Mars."

"Maybe, but nobody ever died in a blowout before. Ever. The airlock was less than ten meters away."

"So he didn't make it."

"I would have. I could move ten meters on a single breath of air, easy. So could you."

"You can't be sure. Maybe he wasn't aware of the break. Maybe he blacked out before he realized there was a problem."

"The skeptical point of view."

"I'm just playing devil's advocate. Anything else?"

She shook her head to fluff her hair. "Sorry, that's all I've got."

Ford didn't want their conversation to look like they were hatching a plot. He turned sideways in his chair and hung an arm over the seatback.

"You're suggesting foul play. Why would anyone want to kill P.L. Scott?" he wondered.

"He was a loose cannon. Seditious. Campaigning to inaugurate a government. He wanted to merge with the Outpost, the settlement up north where anything goes."

"Got evidence of his activities? Anything at all?"

"Just what I heard."

Rooney's eyes were shining warmly under the subdued Food Hall lights. Ford got the message loud and clear.

"You knew him, I guess."

She winced. "Yeah, I did."

Ford drew a breath, expecting the worst. "Pretty well, I bet."

She blushed. "Close personal friends."

"Ouch" — he whistled through his teeth — "My new wife, and the poor guy's widow, don't forget — she know?"

"Probably." Rooney made a face. "Cratertown ain't the biggest city you've ever seen."

Ford nodded, absorbing the news. "Okay, Doc, keep digging, this is quite a problem."

She patted his arm and abruptly stood up to leave.

"Now it's your problem. I'm just a bystander. Take care of Hesperia, she's your lucky charm."

Ford watched her strut away through the noisy throng. He shook his head. That is some babe, he thought. What is she doing here?

▼

Hours passed, and red dawn swiftly erased the stars Ford thought he was watching. He was curled up on a bench in the now empty Food Hall, wrapped in his blanket. He was dreaming.

He and his squad of gringos were scratching through a chilly pine forest east of Mescalero, on the Rez. As the sky brightened behind them they crested a ridge above the tiny village of Tumulo. Ford focused his night vision glasses on the scattered buildings. Behind one of them lurked a hoverjeep. Behind another an armored personnel carrier. In the dirt quadrangle between the adobe chapel and the general store were half a dozen men in combat helmets. *Los Divisores!* He could just make out the crazy jagged stripes on their uniforms. They were setting up a power laser on its heavy tripod. Ford's heart skipped a beat.

He made a motion, and one of his own men passed him the aerodart. Their last one. He hoisted the weapon to his shoulder and trained it on the laser.

"Searching, searching, searching . . ." it murmured softly. Then, "on target, on target, on target . . ."

Ford cranked a lever sharply downward. The missile exploded from its launch tube with a tremendous blast. He watched the fiery exhaust rocketing toward Tumulo, saw *Divisores* try to flee, saw the missile skimming over the treetops, saw it plow into the power laser, saw pieces of metal and bodies flying everywhere, lit with perfect clarity by a wrathful ball of flame.

Then everybody was scrambling. The *Divisor* hoverjeep roared to life, racing toward them. Explosions cut the tops off the trees overhead. A blast at his feet levitated him skyward with magical ease and dropped him into a rotting jail cell. He was there, he knew, awaiting execution. Rifle shots echoed through the adobe walls, signaling death to his squad mates.

"Captain Ford?" growled the *carcelero*, his jailer, leering at him through iron bars. He was carrying something thin and pointed. Ford tried to back away, but the cell was too narrow.

"Brother Ford?" he asked again.

"Don't touch me!" shouted Ford and opened his eyes.

"Wouldn't think of it," said an old man leaning on a broom nearby.

Ford sat up. He looked around at the tables and chairs. A few early risers were filing into the area, ordering hot drinks and pastries.

"Christ, I'm cold. Time?"

"Six thirty. Best go on home now. Unit heaters, they'll warm you up pretty quick."

Ford threw the blanket over his shoulders. He nodded a thank-you, shambled over to the cafeteria, and surveyed the unfamiliar offerings.

"You know Hesperia Dale?" he asked the counterman.

He nodded. "She always orders a Martian Moon and a cup of green tea."

"Two Moons then, please, and tea and coffee."

"Good start," said the counterman with a knowing wink.

Ford ignored the not-so-encouraging words. He presented his handheld to the cash register, and a sum was deducted from his account. He looked around, noting three exits.

"East Side Residence?"

The counterman pointed. Ford tucked his pillow under an arm, took his bagged-up breakfast in one hand, and marched away. He hoped his determined stride signaled the confidence he needed but didn't feel.

▼

When you wanted directions in The Ark, Ford already learned, your handheld showed the way. He recited Dale's address in the Upper East Side Residence Complex, and noted a blinking arrow on his device. It was pointing east along Interplanetary Highway, one of the wider thoroughfares in the habitat. He let out a sigh of relief. After wandering around last night, he would never be able to find his way back home without detailed guidance.

Dale greeted him with a shy smile when he pounded on her door.

"Good morning, Brother Ford."

"It's Joe. Not actually your brother."

"Ooh," she grinned. "Prickly this morning."

"Do I get a kiss?"

She laughed. "Why not?"

She bestowed a quick peck on his cheek and made a sweeping gesture to invite him inside.

"Well . . . that's a start," he said, surprised by the warmish welcome.

She shook a finger. "Don't press your luck . . . Joe."

While they both munched on Martian pastries Ford watched her go to work on her computer. The big screen showed a chair with a curving back and a central pillar for legs. She was pointing a finger to rotate the image around and making small adjustments in the details.

"You're a designer."

"One of my jobs. I did most of the second generation furniture."

"I think I slept on one of your benches."

"Probably."

"And the cafeteria signs? The posters?"

"Mine too."

"Wow, they're pretty good. *You're* pretty good."

"Good enough for Mars, anyway, huh?"

Ford scowled. "I didn't say that. You give the place some individuality. Some real personality."

"Look, she said, swallowing the last of her tea, "I'm due in the studio. We're gearing up to print a prototype today."

She grabbed her purse and bolted for the door.

"Shower's ready."

She pointed over her shoulder as she stepped into the walkway and joined a crowd of pedestrian commuters heading for a hundred different jobs.

"You get one minute max."

8

NILOSYRTIS HOBERMAN, a young and aspiring technician, had Joe Ford's multiprobe spread out in pieces all over the customs lab desk. He was exhausted. He had spent hours at a computer display, browsing through the small square plastic chips where Ford's personal library was stored. He couldn't find anything *subversive.*

Likewise the Earthman's variable wrench. It was what it seemed to be: a simple tool. Now he had disassembled Brother Ford's fancy circuit tester looking for — what? What was Counselor Pomerance worried about? Hoberman couldn't figure it out. The multiprobe was just another tool, like the wrench. Any well-equipped repairman might use one.

Ed Imowelo, his boss, poked at one of the components. "What's this?"

"Looks like a source tracer to me."

"Speak English."

"That's what I'm doing. It performs inverse Fourier transforms of line signals."

"Source tracer." Imowelo nodded doubtfully.

"Gotta be."

"Hmm. And this?"

"Frame buffer. Display stuff for the meter head."

"How do you know?"

"See those little lines? Bar code part numbers."

"Are you sure?"

"Pretty sure," said Hoberman.

"If you're wrong, I'm gonna make you explain it all to the Counselor, understand?"

Pomerance had led Imowelo to believe that the Earthman was suspicious without telling him exactly why. The customs agent dreaded the possibility that he might allow some dangerous goods to fall into the wrong hands. Not that he shared the Counselor's doubts; on the contrary, he thought Joe Ford was a good man. Solid. Truly, a valuable citizen. But he had no desire to be the object of the Counselor's wrath, and he didn't trust young Hoberman's judgment. The electronic specialist was a notorious bonehead.

"Look," said the youth. "This thing is powered by a graphite battery. It puts out maybe a milliwatt. Even if it is some sort of comm unit, it can't transmit across the room. How's he going to reach Earth with it?"

"So you're absolutely positive."

"Well, who knows what they're doing on Big Blue now. I've never been there. Never seen any of their hot stuff. Have you?"

"No."

"So I can't be sure one hundred per cent. But it looks okay."

"All right. We'll turn it over."

▼

At the customs counter Ford watched Imowelo approach. The man looked a little sheepish as he handed over the library and the wrench.

"Sorry we kept them so long. Procedures, you understand."

"Sure."

"Don't worry, we didn't erase anything."

Ford glared at him. "I hope not. Where's my multiprobe?"

"Ahhh." The customs agent turned toward the doorway leading back into the laboratory. "Nilo! Get your ass out here!"

Hoberman scuttled into view, cradling the multiprobe in both hands. "Here you are, Brother," he said, handing the device to

Ford. "Nice piece of equipment."

As the Earthman examined the instrument, the case suddenly came open, dropping parts all over the counter top.

"A-hem." Ford held up the now empty shell. Hoberman blanched under his thatch of blond hair.

"Uh-oh. I thought I had it all stitched together. Hope I didn't blow up the source tracer."

Ford gave the kid a withering look. "The what?"

"You know, the fourier transform chip . . ."

"There's no transform chip. It does direct sampling and linear prediction."

"Oh." Hoberman was mortified.

"You didn't know that. You don't know dot about this thing, and you dared to take it apart?" Ford shook his head in disbelief. How old was this guy? Twenty, twenty-one? Earth years, of course; nine or ten Mars revs. And he was probably Cratertown's electronics whiz. "Do you know how much it would cost to send another one from Earth? Do you have any idea?"

"No, Brother. I don't."

Ford marched righteously around the counter and into the lab. Imowelo and Hoberman timidly followed. They watched as the newcomer arranged the parts on the work bench and expertly reassembled them with the aid of a circuit board pawl and a static charge deflector. When he had the pieces back together, he pressed a key.

After a moment the thing blurted, "Test green . . . test green . . ." in a tinny little voice.

Ford breathed a sigh of relief; the damned thing still worked. He studied the young technician, becoming aware of his injured pride. "Next time, think. I'm backlogged enough already. What else have you screwed up?"

Hoberman felt himself becoming angry. This pig of an Immigrant was being rude on purpose. He started to open his mouth when he felt Imowelo's restraining hand on his shoulder.

"Action in harmony, Brother Ford," said the customs man. "He means well."

Ford shrugged. "Okay. Harmony in thought. When I was a kid, I was a jerk too."

"And thought in action," murmured Hoberman, pale with humiliation.

▼

The Ark's Town Hall was a small dimly lighted room attached to one side of a circular structure that currently served as a storehouse for the Township's public works supplies and equipment. Before that it comprised the office space, living quarters, and headquarters of the entire human presence on Mars. It was the oldest section of Human Habitat One.

Ford sat down in one of a half-dozen comfortable chairs lined up opposite a row of computer terminals complete with flat screens, microphones, and more than two hundred years after their invention, QWERTY keyboards.

He typed his name. The nearest screen lit up.

SHOW IDENTIFICATION

He presented his handheld to an electronic scanner.

WELCOME CITIZEN FORD
STATE SERVICE REQUEST

He leaned toward a microphone. "I'd like to speak to the Town Manager, please. Tammy — that's her call sign, right? I'm looking for an autopsy record."

TOWN MANAGER UNAVAILABLE
TOWN RECORDS UNAVAILABLE

"Well, shit."

CANNOT PROCESS
UNKNOWN COMMAND

"Okay, let's try this — forget Tammy, go command primitive and surface me the death certificate for P.L. Scott — from, say, six months ago . . . or make that seven months to be sure."

PERCIVAL LOWELL SCOTT
SEARCHING

"That's better." He sat back to await the document. And almost immediately the computer responded:

DOCUMENT NOT FOUND
P xxx L xxx S
DEATH RECORD
DOCAGAGAGANOT
R>R>R>R>R
@$#T%@MRD@&%^*!%
#...#...#...#

"What the hell?"

9

THE ARK INFIRMARY housed six beds and Eridania
Rooney's office. Only one of the beds was occupied. The patient's
head was bandaged. An IV drip was delivering a cocktail of
antibiotics and painkillers into one of his wrists. His breathing was
labored. Dr. Rooney triggered the power switch on her portable
vital signs monitor, but the machine failed to display any of its
own vital signs.

"Well, fuck this," she said to herself, and dialed the Township's
Help Desk with an urgent repair request. Nilo Hoberman
answered on the third ring.

"My main monitor is fried, Nilo," she complained.

"Let me triage," said Hoberman, checking his job list.

"I'll do the triaging around here, thanks. I need to see the vital
signs of my patient, who has suffered serious injuries, so I don't
miss any adverse developments. Need this now."

Hoberman was filling in for Ed Imowelo, The Ark's customs
agent, who doubled as its public works dispatcher. He gritted his
teeth and forwarded the call to Joe Ford, who presented himself
to Dr. Rooney with tools in hand.

"Show me the problem, Doc" he said.

"Dana," she reminded him, and demonstrated the monitor's
power failure.

Ford plugged his system analyzer into a socket on the monitor
and read the results off a small display screen.

"Nothing wrong with your babysitter."

He followed the machine's power cord to a wall socket, and
placed his analyzer against it.

"Well, guess what? Power's dead here. Ground fault circuit

protector is what's fried."

"Can you fix it?"

"I'm too new to know" — he scanned his handheld — "database says we have a new one in stock, but I need to fetch it." He shrugged. "That is, if I can find the thing in our warehouse. That place looks like King Tut's tomb."

Rooney smiled. "I have confidence." She patted his arm. "You look like you know what you're doing."

Even in her shapeless white smock, Rooney cut a very sexy figure. Ford was getting a message that sounded like an invitation. He acknowledged it with a wary grin and a little salute.

"Back in a flash. Or as fast as feet can make the trip."

"I'll be waiting," she said. Her voice was warm and throaty.

▼

In the Township warehouse he followed his handheld's directions to Aisle 38, Bin 17, the repository for GFCI power outlets. It was empty.

"Damn."

He looked around for an extension cord. Ten minutes later in Aisle 25, Bin 03, he had one. It was short, but the bin held three of them.

Back in the infirmary he connected the cords together and handed one end to Rooney.

"Here, try your office outlet."

She dragged the cord around the corner and plugged it in behind her desk. Ford then plugged the scanner into the end of the cord he was holding. Chimes and a test pattern signified power returning to the monitor.

Rooney leaned over her patient and glued sensors to his arms and chest. The monitor responded by displaying a steady heartbeat and good oxygenation.

Ford watched her work. The patient was a mess. Eyes swollen shut, blood oozing through the bandage circling his head. Dark bruises on his partially visible torso. Ford's brow wrinkled as he tried to place the messed-up face.

"Oh my God," he blurted. "it's Ed Imowelo."

"Good guess. Quite a sight, huh?"

"How did it happen? Jesus — did he, like, fall off a ladder somewhere?"

Rooney regarded the naïve maintenance man with a sour expression. "He got beat up."

"You're kidding."

"Live and learn, Brother Ford. You're looking at the Active Deacons' handiwork."

"Christ."

"He was distilling alcohol in the rover shop. We both drank some of it, remember?"

"And it's proscribed. Will he be okay?"

"Chances are good. Those boys are pretty careful, teach a lesson, nothing life-threatening."

"How do you know the perps' IDs?"

"You really are new. They brought him in, of course."

Ford whistled tunelessly.

Rooney folded her arms, hugging herself. "Cratertown. What you get when there is no law. Rules, the real rules, and the means of enforcement."

▼

When Joe Ford returned to the tiny apartment in East Residence District, Dale wasn't home. Ford was hoping to see her, but once again she had succeeded in avoiding him. As Buster Mayfield had predicted, Dale was perfectly willing to have Ford share her living quarters, once she had made her point. But in the week since their marriage, social transactions were pretty much down to mumbled good nights and good mornings. She explained the workings of their tiny kitchen and bath, showed him where to find the East Residence laundry, and that was that.

Ford stripped off his clothes, set the timer to one minute, and hopped into the tiny shower stall. The trick was to get wet, turn off the flow while he soaped up, then restart the water and rinse. Ford discovered that he could get wet in under ten seconds, leaving more than forty-five seconds to luxuriate under the drenching hot spray.

The water turned itself off, and Ford padded into the bedroom for clean underwear.

"Brother Ford!"

Dale was standing in the apartment doorway. She blanched and whirled away at the sight of her husband's naked body.

Ford chuckled. "Pardon me." He threw on some clothes. "Okay, I'm decent."

Dale marched to their tiny closet, yanked it open and held out a paper bathrobe. "Next time use this, if you don't mind."

"Whatever you say."

"If we try to be as considerate as possible, then maybe we can get through this."

Ford looked at her quizzically. "Get through this? Get through it to what? What comes next?"

Dale squirmed in confusion. "I . . . I don't know. Nothing. That's not what I meant."

Ford shrugged. He was enjoying her discomfiture. "What did you mean? Divorce? Consummation? What?"

"Just drop it, will you?"

"Glad to," he said.

Dale didn't notice Ford's duffle bags on the floor right away.

They were bulging with clothes and, judging by the bumps and protrusions, other possessions as well.

"Your bags — um, what? What's going on?"

"I decided I don't want to sleep under your dinner table anymore. This marriage . . . it's not working."

"No, it's not. You're a spy."

"Hmm. I'm just another Immigrant — but I'm not a dope — You're Martian counter-intelligence. That's why you agreed to marry me."

Dale reddened. "That's not true, but you don't have to understand, so go ahead, leave. Go back to Earth if you want."

"I'm giving that idea some thought."

"All right, but tell me, why the big move now? Why not yesterday or next week?"

"Well, I hear there's room in the bachelor dorm."

He hefted the duffles, ran his arms through the straps of one to improvise a backpack, and stepped into the corridor. He waved goodbye, and whistling lightly, sauntered off.

Dale picked the groceries out of the little handcart she was towing and slammed them onto the kitchen counter. The man was so arrogant. And, she reflected, hairy too.

10

CENTRAL PARK was enclosed by a wide track built to promote exercise and recreation. At any given time, dozens of citizens of the Independent Republic of Mars could be found walking and running around its five hundred meter length.

Ismenius Pomerance walked around the lake, past the baseball diamond, and across the half-size soccer pitch to the track's on-ramp. There he fell into step with Hadley Timmerman, The Ark's ancient Founder, who was motoring along in his wheelchair. They were in the park for their weekly meeting, out for a stroll to be seen but not overheard by their fellow citizens streaming past.

"What do we do with the Earthman?" asked the Founder.

"Watch and wait, what else?"

"What does our own agent say?"

Pomerance gestured ahead. Coming toward them was Hesperia Dale, running hard. She waved as she flew past.

"Hesper is on our side, but she's unhappy."

"Not going to sway Ford's sympathies toward our enterprise, I take it," said the Founder in his booming artificial voice.

Pomerance clasped his hands behind his back. He stared at the translucent ceiling. "I'm disappointed, but perhaps we were hasty. She's a widow, after all, still in mourning."

The Founder snorted. "I hear the gossip. Word is, P.L. Scott was not a faithful husband, and the marriage was bleak. What is she mourning for?"

"The blow of a loss, Hadley. For God's sake."

Dale had rounded the track and was speeding toward them again. She waved again as she bounded by.

Ismenius chuckled. "If you're worried about sympathy to our

cause, worried about our project to suborn Ford with a honeypot, you can relax."

"How's that?"

"There's another woman. We won't have to do a thing."

"Let nature take its course."

"Yes, sir."

The Founder barked out a genial snatch of laughter.

"I like it."

They continued around the track in silence for a while. Dale rocketed past again, sprinting for an imaginary finish line. She was perspiring. This time she didn't wave.

Pomerance tapped an armrest on the Founder's wheelchair. "About the still . . ."

"Gone, yes? Destroyed, I hope. And Imowelo?"

"He was reprimanded. He will return to duty in a couple of weeks as a wiser man."

"Very good."

"His activities raise an issue, sir. Social pressure. It's building."

"We'll calm it down."

"Yes, of course. Like-Minded solidarity will prevail. However, we must grasp the situation, know what it means. P.L. Scott was a ringleader, but hardly the only dissident. Voices have suggested selling our latest fabrication panels to the Outpost. Maybe we should loosen our reins, make a gesture, what do you think?"

The Founder toggled his joystick. The wheelchair squealed to a sudden stop. "Only if the price is right. But commerce won't appease the dissidents. We've got to talk to some of them."

"Sir?"

"You know, *talk.* Have a conversation. A *serious* conversation. And keep an eye on the Earthman. Understood? "

"Yes, sir. Read you loud and clear."

STEP **TWO**

11

ASPIRING ACTIVE DEACON Nilo Hoberman received a command to appear before The Ark's Counselor without any explanation. That made him nervous as he squeezed himself into Ismenius Pomerance's tiny office.

"Sit down."

Hoberman lowered himself onto a slick plastic chair.

"New furniture?"

Pomerance nodded. "Hesperia's latest. You get to test the prototype."

"It's . . . um . . . comfortable," he said.

"Know why I sent for you?"

"No, sir, I don't. What did I do now?"

"Do? Don't fret, nothing except good work."

Pomerance looked the young man up and down. When he thought about recruits to Ark Service and the Active Deacons squad, he lamented the scarcity of decent candidates. Hoberman was a promising kid, intelligent, responsible, and energetic . . . but, he mused, also soft. He sighed.

"Tell me, you're Like Minded, of course. How do you feel about our society, the Independent Republic of Mars? What do you think about the way we avoid formal organization?"

Hoberman clasped his hands together to keep them from shaking. "Action in Harmony."

Pomerance nodded. "Harmony in Thought."

"And Thought in Action," finished Hoberman.

"Good, good, very good. Now, when you look at our habitat, what do you make of its condition? The state of repair?"

Hoberman shook his head. "Truth, sir?"

74

"Always."

"It needs a lot of work. Most everything is old and worn out, except for things like this chair" — he swallowed hard — "um, the place is falling apart."

"Right you are. I agree. And I have a new assignment for you."

"Okay."

"We — the Founder and I — we want you to become Joseph Ford's apprentice."

"Counselor?"

"He's a trained maintenance engineer."

"He's also a self-important asshole . . . pardon me."

Ismenius grinned. "You've met, I take it."

"Oh yeah."

"Please contain any hard feelings. He's our *only* trained maintenance engineer. We need to go to school on him, build our expertise, have a backup."

"Unh-huh."

"And you're going to be that backup."

▼

Hoberman found Ford in the Town Hall, attempting, without success, to analyze and repair Tammy, the Town Manager.

"Brother Ford?"

The Earthman was crouching under a long bench supporting the room's suite of computer terminals. He detached his multiprobe from a data cable and stood up.

"Yes? Who wants to know?"

"It's Nilo Hoberman."

"Oh, I remember. You managed to take this thing apart" — he brandished the multiprobe — "without actually destroying it."

"Uhh . . ."

"That was good work for someone who never saw equipment

like this before."

Hoberman was ready to be aggressive, but now he relaxed. The Earthman was trying to be nice.

"I'm supposed to go to work for you, be your apprentice."

Ford smiled. "You mean, learn a thing or two."

"I guess so. As an Active Deacon, I take my orders from the Counselor."

Ford rubbed his right hand against his shirt and extended it toward the younger man.

"Well, what do you know? Welcome to the repair team. Now there's two of us on it."

Hoberman grasped Ford's hand. They shook.

The Earthman gestured toward the computer terminals and the big screen where Tammy refused to appear.

"Tammy's down and out. I'm trying to figure out why, but I can't get into the hardware" — he pointed — "behind that door."

"Yeah, well, it's locked."

"And . . . "

"And I have the combo."

"All right, then. Let's take a closer look."

The Town Hall server room was not much bigger than a closet. Three racks containing server blades, each one a specialized computer module, lined one wall. Several of the blades were sitting on the floor, tied into the network by a tangle of cables.

"Sloppy, sloppy, look at this mess," said Ford.

A cabinet holding the power supply equipment stood against a second wall. LED status lights were blinking red, green, and yellow.

Ford snapped a switch on the power supply dashboard. Some of the little lights turned green, others red. "Where's the power coming from? Any idea?"

Hoberman pressed three different switches, and all the lights turned green.

"Main fusor out behind the Town."

"Looks like you know your way around this stuff. Ever have trouble with it? Power surges? Anything?"

"Nope. It's a Traeger Systems installation, genuine article. That stuff is bulletproof."

Ford nodded. "Okay, but the setup in here is so old, the blades don't have standard ports." He placed his multiprobe against each blade, one after another. "Which one holds the executive control?" he wondered.

The first eighteen blades he examined were operating normally. He tried the ones sitting on the floor. Two of the three were also functioning normally, but one of them was not. He pulled a screwdriver from his belt and opened the case. He ran the multiprobe around the now exposed circuit board. He pointed at one of the integrated circuit chips.

"Here's our problem."

"How do you know?"

"Well, my probe is telling me that information is not flowing through the tiny wires inside this thing, see?"

He showed Hoberman the display screen on his instrument.

"Aha! I get it."

"But I don't need the probe to tell me anything in this case."

"No? Why not?"

Ford pointed at the circuit board where the chip was mounted. "What do you see here?"

Hoberman leaned close. "Not much, why?"

"The board is warped, notice that? Tiny bubbles in the plastic. What does that tell you?"

"The chip got hot."

"Right. It melted. And unless I miss my guess, this is where Tammy is hiding. Why she can't talk."

Hoberman opened up his handheld and took a picture. He enlarged the resulting image enough to read a tiny number engraved on the chip's plastic surface. "Before it got busted, this lump used to be a PP-64-80."

"Good. Let's print a new one."

Hoberman groaned. "'Fraid not. The chip printer's busted too."

Ford's lips twisted into a wry grin. "Figures," he said.

He took up the failed blade's cover and was preparing to screw it back in place when he noticed a small detail on the circuit board. He ran a fingertip around the edges of the melted chip. It came away blackened by soot.

"Uh-oh. There's more to this story. What else do you see?"

Hoberman leaned over the circuit board again and stared at it. Then he scratched his head. "Nothing. Melted chip. We need a new one."

Ford pointed to a pair of minute black marks, indentations in the plastic where the chip's fine gold-plated leads connected to the circuit board's wider traces.

"Yeah? What?"

"Looks to me like a high voltage was applied right here. Scorched the surface, melted it, and zapped Tammy."

Hoberman frowned. "Clumsy repair accident, I guess, huh?"

"Or . . ." speculated Ford, ". . . it was deliberate."

"Lord love us."

"You're the Township's computer nerd. Ring a bell?"

"God, no. Who would do a thing like that?"

12

FORD AND HOBERMAN strode along a nearly empty South Promenade after the morning rush hour.

"What are we fixing today, Brother Ford?"

"Let's start with something that people will notice, West Side Auxiliary."

"The death trap."

"That's right. But first, we need some tools and parts."

"Warehouse? I know a shortcut."

Hoberman pointed to an opening on their left and led the way down a narrow passageway. Ford felt the onset of mild claustrophobia cause his heart to thump.

"What is this place?"

"Oh, HVAC service tunnel." Hoberman noted Ford's pallor. "It's okay, we're almost there."

The tunnel ended with the warehouse doors waiting for them on the far side of a much wider corridor.

"Here we are, warehouse!" exclaimed Hoberman. "I'll join up, but now we're down this way, I've got Active Deacon duty in our Media Studio" — he indicated a different set of nearby doors — "right over there. Counselor wants us to inspect all the facilities."

Ford cocked his head in confusion. Then he grinned. "Ahh . . . say hello to Thuvia."

Hoberman's face turned red. "If she's there."

▼

While Ford rummaged through the warehouse, Hoberman had a look around the Media Studio. He could hear faint music coming from an office alcove and a voice humming along with it. He looked inside and there, as hoped, was Thuvia Lofgren. She had headphones clamped over her ears and was typing something on a laptop computer. Her head and shoulders were bobbing to the tune.

"Hey, Thuvia," offered Hoberman.

Lofgren jerked upright. Her knees came up, flipping the cover of her laptop closed. She tore her headphones off.

"Nilo! Jesus, you scared the shit out of me."

Hoberman blanched. "Sorry, not on purpose."

"What are you doing down here?"

"Um Active Deacon crap. Inspecting, Counselor's orders."

"You're kidding."

"Place looks clean. That's what I'll report."

"Well, you better."

She reopened her laptop. The blank screen made her shoulders sag. "Well, damn, there goes my blog."

Hoberman leaned over for a good look. "No no, it's still there. Windows 150 Recovery Tool. Open it."

"Huh?"

"Let me." Hoberman reached past her, and with a few keystrokes brought the text of her latest blog post back to life.

"There you go."

Lofgren scrolled through the pages just to be sure. "Okay, thanks, I guess." She regarded him coolly. "Why are you really here?"

Hoberman stuffed his hands into his pockets. "Um, I was wondering . . . maybe we could have dinner . . . you know, some evening when you're not busy."

Lofgren squinted at him. "With you?"

"Yeah."

"Forget it."

"Uh-oh . . . tell me why?"

"Because I might be in a relationship, that's why."

Nilo cringed. He was crestfallen and embarrassed. Lofgren saw that she had hurt his feelings and bit her lip.

"Geez, Nilo, You're a nice kid, but . . ."

"Hey, I'm an Active Deacon now. Maintenance apprentice. Moving up."

". . . and we used to date, sure, but please — you're *such a boy.*"

▼

A subdued Hoberman found Ford in the warehouse loading a small electric mule with spare parts and equipment.

The Earthman measured his new assistant with narrowed eyes. "You look kind of beat up. Thuvia gave you the brush, yeah?"

"I don't want to talk about it."

"Neither do I. Here's the upside — on you, rejection looks good, makes you seem older."

Hoberman groaned.

Ford bumped his arm with an elbow. "Enjoy your maturity. And while you're at it, take control of our tractor, please."

At the airlock leading into West Side Auxiliary the pair stopped to evacuate the adjoining corridor, to post work signs, and to don pressure suits.

"How long since anyone was in here?" wondered Ford as he wrestled himself into the awkward garment.

"It's been locked off ever since Brother Scott got killed."

"About time to change that, don't you think?"

The airlock door opened and they found themselves in an empty corridor faintly illuminated by sunlight filtered through the haze of its clouded polymer roof. Ford shivered. His suit was made out of rubberized fabric, one thin layer, and meant only for emergency use. Cut off from the heat of the Township for six months, the temperature was fifty degrees below zero. Hoberman, bundled up in the same material, didn't seem to notice. He meandered along the corridor, staring at the ceiling. Half way to the next airlock, he stopped.

"Here's the hole," he said, pointing up at a break in the roof. "What killed poor P.L. Scott."

Working together, Ford and Hoberman unloaded a telescoping pole ladder from the mule and opened its folding legs to steady it against the floor. They worked it back and forth until they were satisfied it was standing right underneath the hole. Ford checked the onboard level to be sure it was pointing straight up, then threw a switch to deploy the ladder, using the mule's battery for power. A sensor on the top end automatically stopped its extension when it touched the ceiling, six full meters above their heads.

"There. Hole in arm's reach," he announced. He threw another switch and rungs unfolded from each side of the pole.

"Hand me that softdisc."

Hoberman held out a shoulder pack containing the repair kit.

Ford put a foot on the lowest rung, grasped a pair of higher rungs with both hands, and started up. In the low Martian gravity, the going was easy. But after just a few steps he paused. The ladder, made out of ultralight carbon fiber, was swaying . He was starting to feel queasy.

Hoberman smiled at the Earthman's discomfort.

"Hey, Dad, come on back down and let me get up there."

Ford winced, embarrassed to be called out by the kid he was supposed to be training. He looked down at Hoberman, then craned his neck to view the hole. It looked like a long way up.

"Well — ?"

Ford didn't reply, but he lowered himself to the floor and handed the pack to Hoberman. He armwaved a be-my-guest gesture and stood aside.

His apprentice rapidly climbed all the way to the ceiling without a qualm, annoying his newly-appointed mentor. Once there he removed the softdisc and dropped the empty shoulder pack. Ford caught it while it was floating down.

"Tie on, Kid," said Ford, gritting his teeth.

Hoberman lashed himself to the pole. He kneaded the rubbery softdisc like bread dough to warm it up. After a minute it started to swell and blister. He jammed it into the hole, where it expanded to seal the break.

They both watched while the gooey material solidified. Hoberman pressed a finger against the repair to test it, then swiftly descended to the corridor floor.

"Airtight now, Brother," said he.

They collapsed the ladder and returned it to the mule. On their way to the far airlock Hoberman stopped short. He pointed at the floor.

"Hey — here's where the death rock hit."

Sure enough, he was pointing at a dent thirty centimeters wide and fifteen centimeters deep.

Ford probed the little bowl with a toe.

"Bent, but not broken. What's the floor made of?"

Hoberman shrugged. "Synthetic something or other. Built long before my time." He scanned the area.

"Um, no rock."

"Maybe it shattered."

Hoberman strode across the corridor and lifted a small object from the floor.

"Nope. Take a look."

He held up a small stone the size of his fist. Part of the surface was intact, still showing a blackened crust from the heat of entry through Mars' thin atmosphere. Where the crust was missing, the interior was perforated by gas bubbles that had burst.

They both oohed and ahhed over the find.

▼

Later toward evening, Ford led Hoberman into the Main Street Food Hall for debriefing and a casual meal.

The assembled citizens, many of whom had already tested the West Side Auxiliary repair by parading through the reopened corridor, clapped and cheered their appearance.

Hoberman pretended not to notice. Ford waved and made a little bow to acknowledge the praise.

They sat down to plant-based burgers and drinks that tasted like root beer.

"Don't be a wallflower, Kid. You just did something important. You won't get many moments like this."

"No applause for a regular day's work, huh?"

"Not where I come from."

They ate in silence while Ford toyed with his plastic fork. One of the tines was missing. The plate cradling his french fries was cracked.

"I'm starting to see a pattern, he said. The Ark? Leaky boat."

"You noticed."

"I did. And it all seems excessive, given your modern materials, your planetary code requirements. What do you make of it?"

Hoberman stared at his food. "No one cares."

"I take that to mean you care."

"Maybe."

Ford regarded his apprentice with a sympathetic smile. "You seem to know a thing or two. Go to school?"

"UCLA remote learning. Radio hell, but I got my BA."

"Good for you. Here's a question: know of any other meteor strikes on the habitat?"

Hoberman shook his head. "None. Tammy might have logged something."

"If only we could query Tammy."

"Yeah, if only. Welcome to Cratertown."

13

NORTH AXIS PROMENADE was packed with people making their afternoon hike back to the residence wings. With a few weeks' practice under his belt, Ford dodged through them as skillfully as if he'd been doing it all his life. As he passed Hundred Yard Market, one of the little second-hand stores that flourished everywhere in The Ark, he was surprised to see Dale. Before he could call her name she snapped, "What are you doing here?"

Ford held up his variable wrench. "Rover oil leak. Ed Imowelo writes the orders, and I obey."

"Hmmph," she sniffed.

"You?"

"Shopping. Trying to find something I haven't seen before."

She held up a trim blue blouse, somewhat faded from many washings.

"What do you think?"

He shrugged. "Looks okay to me. It's nice."

"What am I thinking of? I don't need it."

She hung the blouse back on the rack and walked away, heading south.

"Wait!" Ford called after her, but she was already out of earshot and lost in the crowd.

As he neared North Perimeter, the crush thinned. He stopped outside the Freight Vehicle Repair Station and looked around. As far as he could see the coast was clear in both directions. Satisfied, he opened the door and stepped inside.

Ford checked his repair order. He was looking for Township Freight Transporter Number 303. There it was, sitting forlornly near the far wall of the garage, motor casing open, transmission oil dripping onto the concrete floor. He found a shop trolley, stretched out on it, and rolled himself under the sorry-looking vehicle.

The problem was obvious. The main drive pinion was stripped. This Ford had anticipated; it was a common flaw in older General Electric drivetrains. He carefully unwrapped a re-machined gear and placed it on the floor beside his head. He made no further attempt at repair, however. Instead he pulled out his multiprobe, plugged in a pair of wire leads, and attached the alligator clips dangling from them to the battery charger sitting beside the truck. He jammed a tiny transducer into his ear, tapped a sequence of numbers on the multiprobe keypad and waited.

For a long while, nothing happened. It was like listening to the sea in a seashell. Then, very faintly, a voice swam up out of the noise . . .

> *Hello, Blue Eyes. Squawk channel six-four-zero one time and tell us your story. Two-way delay is three-niner minutes as of oh-two-twenty-one.*

Ford punched the numbers six, four, zero on his keypad. Then, holding the probe close to his mouth, he whispered his report.

> *Hello, BlueTalk. Agent in place. Working per assigned cover. Local situation conforms to prior simulations. Investigating possible singleton homicide as alleged by Background Man, whose ID as it happens, is local physician Eridania Rooney, an Earther like me.*

Ford's earpiece crackled with an incoming transmission, a message sent half an hour before his own report. He listened intently to some dire news. When it ended he lay back to consider its import. His body wasn't moving, but his mind was racing.

After a few minutes of anxious uncertainty, he thought he knew
how to reply:

> *Stand down for now. My status is suspected, but we
> knew that would happen. I have freedom of action. No
> immediate danger. Trying to persuade local authorities
> — such as they are — to engage. No joy yet. Social
> cohesion is not threatened, although, on a personal note,
> my new wife doesn't love me.*

As he spoke, a pair of legs appeared in the doorway. They
moved quietly and purposefully toward Transporter Number 303.
Concentrating all his energy on the radio link, Ford never heard
them approach.

> *Uh-oh, BlueTalk, starting to fade. Tell Bobber: Mars
> gravity is great, but the food here is terrible . . .*

A pair of hands reached down, grabbed him around the ankles
and yanked. The Earthman came scooting out from under the
rover on his little trolley. Standing over him was Hesperia Dale,
her face hot with furious outrage.

"What in the name of Heaven do you think you're doing!?"

Ford made no attempt to stand up. "Phoning home. What does
it looks like?"

"I see — you're homesick."

Ford unplugged the multiprobe leads from the battery charger.
"That's what a bad marriage will do for you."

"You miserable shit. We took you in! We made you a citizen!"

Ford slowly got to his feet. Dale let him stand, then hauled off
and slapped him across the face. The force of her swing threw her
off balance, and she jigged sideways a couple of steps.

"Ouch." Ford rubbed his jaw.

"A fucking spy! And you denied it. I asked you point-blank, and you said, *no.* Liar! Ismenius was right!"

"I'm not a liar. Not a spy, either."

"Don't apologize. I don't want to hear it, you bastard!"

She clawed at her left hand, trying to remove the wedding ring Ford had placed there. Very firmly, Ford clamped both his hands over hers.

"Let go, you're hurting me!"

"Calm down. Then I will."

"Fuck you!" She struggled to get free, but Ford was too strong for her. She began to sob.

"Hey, hey — take it easy." He released her and ceremonially opened a hand.

"Six months! P.L. hasn't been gone six months, and I've been living with a goddam spook!"

She tugged the ring from her finger and dropped it into his palm. Ford tossed it into the air, caught it with his other hand, and carefully slipped it into a pocket.

"Spies steal secrets because they want to weaken their enemies. I'm here because I want to strengthen you people."

"Oh, you're not scum, you're the noble savior of humanity."

"Will you listen to me?"

Dale regarded him icily, then spun on her heel and headed for the door.

"Wait" — he held up his multiprobe — "Know what this is?"

"Your damn spy radio, I guess."

"That's right. But without some external power it can't transmit around the block. Even with the battery charger, I can't reach Earth. Here's my secret" — he pointed toward the heavens above — "up there, a thousand miles above Phobos, we've got a satellite relay in orbit. It's been here longer than I have."

"Am I supposed to be impressed?"

"You decide. For some reason, I trust you. Tell the Counselor if you want. But first, have a listen to the message my probe decoded from BlueTalk."

"BlueTalk?"

"My contact back on Earth."

He switched on the multiprobe's tiny speaker and replayed the incoming transmission:

> Be advised, Blue Eyes, PSA executive committee has authorized formation of a planetary task force. If situation deteriorates, we are prepared to launch police battalion on fast track to stabilize errant colony.

Dale balled up her fists. "They wouldn't dare."

"Don't be too sure. Let me do my work, and you won't have anything to worry about."

"Blackmail — you've got nerve!"

"Fine point," he corrected with a smile. "Technically, it's extortion."

"Rest easy, I'm not going to turn you in. Ismenius doesn't need my help, and he's not going to get it.

She shook a finger at him and stalked off with a parting shot:

"Your eyes are brown, for God's sake."

14

ED IMOWELO offered a vacant storage bay in a corner of the rover shop to serve as an office for Ford and Hoberman. They were going over their schedule for the day when Zoran Boskovoy appeared with a high-priority ticket that trumped their plans.

"We've got a telescope? Who knew?" marveled Ford.

"Up on the mesa just beyond the airport," said Boskovoy. "And it's covered with dust."

Ford checked his computer.

"Says here that it's equipped with a blower. What's the problem?"

Boskovoy sat himself down on a crate.

"The blower quit."

"And you want us to fix it."

"Please. I need to complete a project and write it up."

Ford scowled. "Is it safe out there today?"

Hoberman turned to the daily weather report.

"Winds are light. Air is minus five at noon. Thermal bleed is minimal, so jackets are all we need for cover in the car. Old Sol is being nice, no flares, radiation danger flag is green. Still got to wear our tags, but it's safe enough. We can go."

Ford shrugged. "Better requisition a ride."

Hoberman checked a Township database.

"Gee, Brother, the only available rover today is a two seater."

"Better grab it."

Hoberman pressed some keys.

"Done."

Boskovoy cleared his throat. "I need to be in the rover."

"What?"

"Gotta oversee the repair. Science protocol. The scope is my responsibility."

Ford nodded. "Okay, then. Nilo, looks like you're excused."

Hoberman shrugged. "Fine by me. How about I take a look at our chip printer?"

"Good idea."

▼

Ford found a blower motor in Aisle 19, Bin 24 of the Township warehouse. It was rattling around behind the rover seats as Ford and Boskovoy trundled out of the North Portal airlock in Township Rover Vehicle Number Nine and bounced over rocks and sand on the road leading to the ferry terminal.

Ford examined the tag pinned to his EVA pressure suit.

"How do I read this thing?"

The rover was designed with large polymer windows in front, back, and overhead. To Ford the vehicle seemed awfully open, an invitation to the distant Sun's electromagnetic wrath.

Boskovoy smiled. "Don't worry. Sun is quiescent these days, at the low point in its cycle. No sunspots, no flares. We're okay."

"I don't feel okay."

"First excursion jitters."

Ford let out a sigh and tightened his grip on the control yoke, getting a feel for rover performance. Boskovoy studied his nervous traveling companion with a twinkle in his eye.

"Hey, Joe, get a grip. Let me tell you why I waited until the only rover available had just two seats."

"You see the roster?"

"Checked it every day for a week. I thought you might want to hear about your new apprentice from another Earther."

This idea overrode Ford's fear of solar radiation.

"Tell me."

"Well, he's one of the Active Deacons. No real government, here, but maybe you already know how things actually work."

"You mean, like what happened to Imowelo."

"You got it. Hoberman works for the Counselor. He's keeping an eye on you for that stuffed shirt Pomerance."

"I kind of figured as much. There's not much to tell."

Boskovoy interrupted himself to consult his handheld. "Wait, we're close." He pointed out the forward window.

"Hang a left here. Head for the mesa."

Ford turned off what passed for the main road, drove north for a kilometer, then guided the rover slowly up a narrow track onto a plateau that rose steeply out of the Klickitat Crater floor. There before them a spidery titanium structure loomed out of the dusty air.

"Here we are, Brother. Scope City."

Ford parked beside a concrete pillar supporting the thing. He took note of the two-meter mirror held aloft by a web of titanium struts. On Earth the instrument would tumble down in the slightest breeze, but here on Mars whose gravity was only three-eighths as powerful , he had to admire the daring design.

"What good is it? You know, with all the orbiting platforms we've got."

Boskovoy handed Ford the blower replacement.

"Well, when first built it was cutting edge. Now it's obsolete. No astrophysics breakthroughs, that's for sure."

Ford stared doubtfully at the slender ladder attached to the concrete support pillar. It looked like a long climb.

"So lame, no one else tries to steal your time on it."

"Exactabingo. I'm studying a star that's a big sister to the Sun called HD162826. Perfect target for this hulk — its just a hundred and ten light years away in the constellation Hercules."

He whirled his hands around each other, stirring up an imaginary cloud of gas and dust.

"Billions of years ago, both stars were born in the same stellar nursery. Now I think there's a planet out there a lot like ours. Clean up my mirror, and maybe we'll know for sure."

Ford and Boskovoy checked each other's helmets to be sure they were sealed up tight. When they were satisfied, Ford threw a lever, and a hidden pump withdrew the air inside the vehicle into an onboard storage tank. He dropped the blower replacement and a handful of tools into a shoulder bag, popped the rover door, and stepped out onto the Martian surface. The dusty air, thin as it was, obscured Klickitat's rim twenty kilometers away to the west, but overhead the sky was almost black.

Ford trudged across the sandy plateau to the telescope, paying close attention to the pebbles crunching under his feet. He was anxious about EVA risks and wished he had taken one of his tranquilizer pills before setting out. Yet he felt as light as a feather in the low Martian gravity, momentarily free of The Ark's tightly closed spaces.

"Yahooo," he shouted, elated by his daring outside adventure.

At the base of the telescope he examined the ladder. It looked old. How old? He gave it a tug to prove it was securely fastened to the pillar. A flurry of dust exploded from the rungs, but it seemed solid.

"Going up," he reported.

Boskovoy watched Ford's cautious progress from the comfort of his rover seat. "Okay, you're there. Look for the service package under the mirror."

Ford opened a communications app on his handheld. "Does the scope have a wake word?"

"Nancy." Replied Boskovoy.

"Okay — hey there, Nancy," Ford commanded, "blow dust."

"Sorry, I can't do that. My blower motor is not responding."

"Well, at least your voice box is still in working order."

The EVA pressure suit was bulky and its thick gloves made Ford clumsy. It took him the better part of two hours to open a panel on the service box, find the blower, swap out the failed motor, and test the replacement. When the last screw was screwed back into place, he reopened the comm app on his handheld.

"Nancy, dear," he commanded, "blow dust."

"Blowing dust," replied the telescope's voice module.

Boskovoy checked the results on his handheld. After the new motor had been running for fifteen minutes, he noticed that the dust wasn't clearing.

Ford clambered up onto a narrow platform behind the mirror and reached over the top to clean the blower jets with a brush he dug out of his tool bag.

Another fifteen minutes went by while he watched to make sure the blower actually removed the accumulated layer of dust.

"How we doing, Zoran?"

Boskovoy leaned toward the window and stuck his thumb up. Ford returned the gesture, descended to the ground, and shuffled back to the rover.

Inside, he sealed the door and repressurized the rover's little cabin. They removed their helmets.

"First EVA," said Boskovoy. He punched Ford's arm. "Congratulations, Bro. Mission accomplished."

Ford was sweating in his suit. "Jesus. That was something. Let's go home."

▼

Three kliks down the road, Boskovoy pointed to a knobby hill jutting out of the crater basin. "Over this way. Little side trip."

"What now? I'm beat."

"You can relax in comfort. I'm hunting fossils."

"You're kidding."

"We know life started here, but I think it might have evolved into multi-celled critters . . . say about two billion years ago."

They pulled up beside a rocky outcrop. After the necessary EVA prep, Boskovoy got out and hammered carefully selected pieces of stone loose from the layers of sediment.

"Looks pretty dead to me," said Ford.

Boskovoy shook his head. "Life is tricky, Joe. It's got lots of resources. The will to survive, to bend to prevailing conditions, to dominate."

"If you say so," groaned Ford.

"That goes for us humans, too. Be wary, my friend. That kid Hoberman may be more than just your dutiful assistant."

"What?"

"Hoberman was most likely involved with P.L. Scott's untimely demise."

"Are you drunk or something? Anoxia? Air flowing okay?"

Boskovoy returned to the rover with a sack full of stone shards. He triumphantly pointed out several carbonate inclusions, but Ford was interested in something else.

"You knew this guy Scott?"

"We were pals."

"Everyone here is deeply religious. Why would anyone want to kill him?"

"Because they're fanatics. Because of his political views."

"Come on, that's not so heinous."

Boskovoy snorted. "Well it is if you're in a colony of the Like Minded, and you're publishing broadsides to form a government, legalize booze and dope, merge with the Outpost, where I spend most of my time."

"Yes, that might do it. How do I know such broadsides exist?"

Boskovoy labeled each of his stones with a marker and sealed them all in plastic wrap.

"P.L. had a stash. Where? Not sure. There's a public locker wall, but you didn't hear that from me."

▼

The garage airlock was closed when they returned to the Township. Radio calls to open it went unanswered, so they parked outside and hiked to an airlock on the west side.

On the way, Ford noticed a series of small divots in the sand and something lying in the last one. He bent down and picked it up.

"Would you look at this? A baseball. A baseball on Mars."

Boskovoy hefted it. "Kids. When space weather cooperates, they like to get outside, have some fun."

"Amazing. You can see where it bounced."

Ford dropped the ball into his shoulder bag.

"Uh-oh, I don't feel so good."

He staggered sideways and sank to his knees.

Boskovoy hurried over and picked him up.

"Christ, Joe — your tag is black."

15

DR. ROONEY was updating her patient database when Joe Ford appeared in her office supported by Zoran Boskovoy, who had Ford's left arm draped across his shoulders. Ford's face was white. Both men were still wearing their pressure suits.

Rooney jumped out of her chair and examined Ford's radiation dosage monitor.

"Oh my God. Look at your tag. How long were you out there?"

Ford mumbled something unintelligible.

"Two, two and a half hours outside the rover," said Boskovoy. "He was fixing the telescope."

"Help me get him inside."

Together they maneuvered Ford into the infirmary's patient ward and laid him down on one of the hospital beds. Ford's eyes closed the moment his head hit the pillow.

"Okay, Joe. I'm admitting you. You've taken a pretty good radiation dose, but you're going to be fine."

Ford's eyelids fluttered. He groaned.

"Joe? Can you hear me? Damn, let's get the suit off."

Rooney and Boskovoy unzipped Ford's suit, tugged this way and pulled that way to remove it.

Rooney set up an IV drip and expertly inserted a cannula into Ford's right wrist. She removed a vial from her refrigerator and connected it to the drip line.

"Whatcha got there?" queried Boskovoy.

"Heat shock protein cocktail — temporary immune enhancer.

"Oh . . ."

"Look, Zoran, I got this. Thanks for bringing him in."

Boskovoy nodded to her authority.

"Good night, then, Doc. Like an update when you've got one."

"Yup."

▼

Hours later Rooney returned to Ford's bedside to find him staring at the ceiling. At her approach he attempted to sit up. She gently pushed him back down.

"Don't even think about it."

"Radiation? How much?" he inquired. His words were slurred. "How worried should I be?"

Rooney sat herself down on the edge of the bed.

"Back on Big Blue — were you modified?"

"No, it's not standard practice yet, you know that."

"Well it is here. Zoran should have known better than let you cook in the Sun. Now you've got a cancer risk. You need to get edited."

"Beg pardon?"

"You — Mr. Earth Human — have one copy of $p53$, a primary anti-cancer gene. Elephants, who almost never get cancer, have twenty copies. I'm going to administer a treatment that will give you at least ten copies."

"How dangerous is that?"

"Compared to cancer? Zip. All of the colonists have undergone the treatment. Now it's your turn."

"Well, okay."

"Here's the thing. It's an injection. Harmless virus that carries the molecular tools to open up selected immune cells and add the new genes."

"Wow."

"Only problem is, you will probably be sick for a few days."

Ford scowled, thinking it over.

"Have at it, Doc," he decided.

She patted his cheek.

"Good boy."

▼

Ford slept almost all the time for the next week. Rooney's virus may have been harmless, but it made Ford's body work hard enough to keep him in a perpetual state of exhaustion.

Rooney kept a close watch while he slept. On the third day she was joined by Hesperia Dale, who heard of Ford's difficulties from Nilo Hoberman.

"How's he doing?" asked Dale, worried in spite of herself.

"He's manufacturing new genes, and that's a big load on his metabolism. But he'll be fine."

"Glad of that. I know you're taking good care of him."

"Oh yes. I am." She eyed her visitor. "Sorry if you think we're involved, Hesper. We're not."

Dale heard the doctor's obvious interest. She waved an arm dismissively.

"He's yours, Doc."

"You sure? I'm asking because, you know — P.L., et cetera, et cetera, and so forth."

"I know all about it. You could have him too, for all I cared."

The remark jolted Rooney, who clocked something grim and sad behind Dale's eyes. "Whoa, Hes, you okay?"

"Don't worry yourself. That marriage didn't work either."

▼

On day eight Ford's eyes flew open. After a week of torpor he felt a sudden burst of energy. He sat upright and looked around. He was still the only patient in the ward, a swarthy Earthman in a white room full of white beds and white appliances.

He glanced at the patient monitor beside his bed. The little green lines were spiking with easy regularity. After taking note of his vital signs — blood pressure 125 over 70; oxygen, 99%; Heartbeat, 60 bpm — he removed the leads from his arm, his chest, and his right index finger.

A robe was draped over the rail of the adjacent bed. He put it on and stepped out into the hallway. There, hearing voices, he paused. One of them belonged to Rooney. The other one, younger, tremulous, higher pitched, was hard to place. Then he remembered . . . oh yeah, that podcaster kid. What's her name?

"Thuvia, we need to figure this out. When did you get your last period?"

"Oh God, a month ago. Month and a half, probably. Maybe two?"

"Not this cycle though, it seems. Well, that's a clue, and these days we can do a test right here in my office, take thirty seconds. Bite down on this stick."

"Ow long oo bide?"

"You're done. And the stick . . . the stick has turned purple."

"Oh no."

"Oh yes. You are pregnant, my dear."

Ford heard a tearful shriek.

"Hey, hey, it's okay, you're young, in good health, everything is going to go just perfectly."

"No it's not. I'm not married."

"That won't slow nature down one bit."

Ford heard sobs.

"Talk to the father."

"I can't. We aren't on speaking terms."

"Whoa Nelly — were you raped?"

More sobs.

"No, it was heat of the moment, but I never thought . . ."

"Listen, Thuvia. You have to inform the father. The Like

Minded have this rule . . ."

Another shriek. Chair legs scraped against a hard floor, and footsteps pounded toward the infirmary exit.

Ford waited tactfully for a moment, then rounded the corner into Rooney's office.

"Hey, Doc. Where's my clothes?"

▼

Rooney studied the results of a blood draw on her handheld. She looked across her tiny desk at Ford, who was now dressed, and turned her screen around so he could read it.

"Greek to me," he said. "What's the verdict?"

Rooney smiled.

"Everything looks good. Your immune cells got the upgrade we planned. Be of very good cheer, Joe — as of now you are bulletproof."

Ford grunted his thanks.

Rooney placed a hand on his brow to check his temperature. "Now that you're back to normal, we have to discuss my fee."

"I have to pay?" Ford readied himself to navigate a tricky social situation he saw coming.

"Of course," she grinned. "But my services are cheap. I just need a small favor."

"Name it."

"My printer hasn't worked for months. All these damn PDFs I've been making — I want paper."

Ford relaxed. "I'll take a look."

Rooney opened a cabinet door to reveal an ancient inkjet printer. Ford opened the cover shell, removed the sheet feeder, removed the print head track, removed the print head.

Rooney hovered at his shoulder. He could feel her breath on his neck.

"How's it going with Hesperia?" she asked. "She was standing watch for a while."

"Really?"

"She seemed very concerned."

Ford considered the news. He wasn't ready to discuss his personal problems.

"She's tough, independent, we're working on stuff."

"If you need some help with that — your *stuff* — let me know."

Ford connected his multiprobe to a diagnostic socket on the printer's motherboard.

"Okay, the jet controller . . . now that is one dead soldier."

"Buy me a new one? I'll buy you a drink." — she giggled like a schoolgirl — "Medicinal alcohol pairs well with our native strawberry juice."

Ford couldn't help admiring the woman's wonderful bravado. He also heard an interesting suggestion.

"Let me see what I can do."

16

THE RIO GRANDE was running low in late fall. Joe Ford and his combat patrol squad waded through the shallows and set out eastward across an arid plain, burdened down like mules with packs and aerodarts and assault rifles. As they marched through the mesquite, dodging the chollas, *Divisor* missiles rocketed past them. They hit the dirt. When it was clear they weren't the target, they stood up to glimpse fireballs blossoming in the faraway hills.

A jail door clanged shut. Ford rattled the bars. The *carcelero* approached. What's that in his hand?

"Ahhh — !"

Ford jerked upright on his bachelor bunk. Oof, safe. Not even on the same planet. He was sweating. He ran his hands through his hair, breathed slowly in and out.

Three beds away, the only nearby sleeper stirred. "Hey, pal, quiet down, will ya? I'm still on the shuteye shift."

"Sorry."

Ford opened a little bottle and counted his tranquilizer pills. Three left. He popped one into his mouth, chewed and swallowed. Then he threw the last two away and dressed himself for work.

▼

Nilo Hoberman knew where to find the Township's public lockers and led Ford to them.

"Feeling better? Doctor fix you up okay?"

"I'm a new man, Nilo."

He examined the stacks of lockers set up in long rows separated by narrow aisles. Lord, there were more of them lined up than he ever saw at Disney Galaxy on his only visit.

"Any idea which one of these belonged to P.L. Scott?"

Hoberman shook his head. "Not a chance, Brother." He pondered the problem. "But maybe Hesperia knows. What are we looking for, anyway?"

"Oh, handbills, posters. Political flyers."

"No idea."

"You never saw anything like that? Taking up wall space in the Food Hall, for example?"

"No. Not that I recall."

Ford exhaled an exasperated sigh. He would have to go to his new wife — and now ex — hat in hand.

"Well, then, I better talk to my fair lady. Piece of advice, Nilo — when the time comes, avoid an arranged marriage like the plague itself."

"Sir?"

▼

Out on the Farm Hesperia Dale was patrolling the protein crops. Halfway along a line of leafy poultry bushes, she came to a halt. Among the ripening fruits, the botanical analogs of chicken breasts, several were missing. She was aghast at the obvious vandalism.

"Holy *unbelievable,*" she growled.

She moved on to inspect the traditional nuts and berries, now with sharp eyes scanning every plant. And there she spotted missing raspberries.

"Be damned!"

Someone was stealing food. Who would be so bold? Or so unaccountably desperate?

Not far away, the door to a utility shed standing between the olive grove and the peach trees was open a crack. Dale cautiously stuck her head inside.

"Hello?"

No answer. After a few seconds, Dale's eyes adjusted to the dimly lit interior, and now she saw a young woman huddling in the corner behind the rakes and shovels. Her clothes were filthy, and her face was smeared with dirty tears.

"Thuvia Lofgren! What in the world are you doing here?"

"I don't want anyone to see me," moaned Lofgren.

"Oh? Why not?"

"Especially not the father."

"Thuvia, dear, what are you talking about?"

"We're not together. He's old enough to be my own father."

"Who?"

"My secret."

"This man . . . whoever he is . . . did he hurt you?"

"No. He's okay, but he will worry and come after me when he finds out."

"What's he going to find out?"

"Can't tell you."

Dale placed impatient fists on her hips. "Well, I can't have you stealing food, and you can't hide out here. You have to — "

Before she could finish her command, Lofgren was on her feet. She brushed past Dale and was out the door without so much as a parting nod.

Dale dismissed her with a sardonic wave. "You could have thanked me for the food, you know . . . *sheesh."*

A few minutes later Brother Ford found her documenting the crop losses on her handheld.

"Afternoon, Hesper . . . got a minute?"

Dale spun around with a yelp. "Oh God — *you!* — you startled me."

"Sorry, didn't mean to."

Dale tossed her head. This guy, so sure of himself. What now? She couldn't resist the chance to nurse a grudge. "What brings our blackmailing spy out into the countryside today?"

"Please, Hes, let's move on. I need some information."

"Why should I help you wreck our town?"

Ford rolled his eyes. "That's not my plan. So let's try, *out of the goodness of your heart* — how's that?"

Dale crossed her arms. "All right, I'm listening."

Ford nodded his gratitude. "Your deceased husband had a locker, I'm told. I can't find it."

"Why do you need it?"

Ford stirred the dirt under his feet with a toe. "You think I'm a spy. I'm not. But I am a *detective.* P.L. Scott's death is starting to look like it might be . . . interesting."

Dale swept away a wisp of hair. "And you think the locker contains evidence of some kind."

Ford smiled. "You got it."

Dale took a moment to trim a few loose branches on the nearest raspberry bush with her garden shears.

"Well . . ."

"Forget the public locker bay. Look in the rover shop where he sometimes worked. Dial 25-15-5."

"25-15-5. Thank you."

Ford tapped the numbers into a note on his handheld and turned to go.

"Wait, tell me what you think . . ."

Dale picked a ripe raspberry off the bush and held it out. Ford moved to take it, and she slipped it past his outstretched fingers into his mouth.

He chewed thoughtfully. "Delicious," he decided and made a little salute. "Our farmer has a green thumb."

"See you."
"Take care."

▼

Ford worked his way through the Rover Shop weaving between
the dusty vehicles in need of repair until he found a workbench in
a narrow bay tucked away off the main floor. There among the
wrenches and spare parts he discovered a small safe with a digital
keypad embedded in the door.

Ford consulted his handheld for Dale's combination. Ah yes,
25-15-5. He pressed a key, but then noticed that he didn't need to
unlock the safe. Someone had already found it and pried it open.
Lying on the bench nearby was an oversize screwdriver. Hmm,
the probable instrument of unauthorized entry. He bent a finger
under the door's warped edge and tugged it open.

Inside, what was once a thick stack of handbills had been
reduced to ash. He poked at the flaky pile. The only visible text
on display was a barely discernible headline:

LIKE MI DED CITIZE S !

Ford rubbed his blackened fingers together and cleaned them
with a towel hanging on the wall.

"Well now, what have we got here? A fire? Acid? Looks like
P.L. Scott ran into some heavy censorship."

Just to be sure, he tried the digital combination on the open
door. Lights flashed and the deadbolt retracted.

"Definitely P.L.'s locker," he mused. "And proof enough that
someone didn't like his style."

17

WHILE **WAITING** to pay for bad coffee and a plausible scone in the Barsoomian Bakery fronting on South Prom, Joe Ford observed the young podcasting journalist — what's her name again? — Thuvia, right? — drop three apple fritters into a bag and dart away down the street without actually buying them. What's with that girl? Doesn't Township Television pay their employees?

He showed his own purchases to the squarish little paybot.

ding — "Coffee," — *ding* — "Scone," it said. "Thirty five maroons."

Ford had yet to grasp the full meaning of the local currency. He did a calculation in his head, arriving at the sum of fifty dollars or so. He bit into his scone. The morning's snack was cheaper than anything he could buy on Big Blue.

▼

Ford found Nilo Hoberman waiting for him when he arrived in The Ark's Town Hall, ready to knock off another day's repair tickets.

"I moved the Town Manager to a different blade, Joe, one that still works," he announced.

"*Joe* is it now? What happened to Brother Ford?"

Hoberman winced. "Sorry, I shouldn't be so familiar."

"Not at all . . . *Nilo.* Keep it up, I like names."

"Okay, then, let's see if Tammy got her voice back."

Their experiment was interrupted by Zoran Boskovoy, who stuck his head in the door. Spotting Ford and his apprentice, he came all the way inside.

"Hey, Joe — have you seen Thuvia?"

Ford's eyebrows shot up. "As a matter of fact. Getting coffee at the Bakery— she was hanging around, and then she stole some pastries. Apple fritters, I think."

Boskovoy nodded. "When was this?"

"Just now, this morning. What's the problem? You look like shit."

"I'm all right. I need to talk to her, that's all. She missed her show yesterday."

"Well, she's not here."

"If you do run into her again, have her get in touch."

"Will do. Get some sleep, okay?"

Boskovoy waved his arms in frustration and left to continue his search.

Hoberman gritted his teeth. "Boskovoy! So that's who it is."

"Who is what?"

"Thuvia has a boyfriend. She wouldn't tell me who, but now we know."

"Jesus. Zoran is forty or more, twice her age."

Hoberman considered the idea. "So, twenty-three or so, and she's just twelve, Mars years. He could be her *dad,* for the love of God."

Their discussion was cut short by the voice of the Town Manager. "Name please. Access requires citizen sign-in. Sign in with your name. Name. *Name, name, name.*"

"Hey, Tammy, calm down," said Hoberman, alarmed by her behavior. "It's me, Nilosyrtis Hoberman, and Joseph Ford."

"Name . . . name . . . welcome to The Ark, gentlemen."

"Whoa, that's better."

Ford glanced at some notes on his handheld. "Hey, there, Tammy, open up whatever you've got on Percival Lowell Scott, please. Dossier, personal documents . . . autopsy is a priority."

"Priority. Priorities. Prioritize. Priory. *Auto-prio-zazzzz . . .*"

"What was that — ?"

Hoberman scratched his head. "She's got some vocabulary, but she's disconnected from her databank."

"I'll say." — Ford shook his head in professional despair — "How does The Ark manage to stay afloat with your Town Manager in this kind of shape?"

"She's only been out of action for a few months. Nothing has come up that really demands her attention, and we ordered a new executive module from Earth. Should be here on the next cycle ship."

"I see," said Ford. "How many months, you say?"

"I think six."

"From about the time of P.L. Scott's death then."

Hoberman looked very uncomfortable. "Now that you mention it . . . just about."

▼

Ford paid a visit to Ed Imowelo in the mechanic's customs shed. The man still wore a bandage over his left eyebrow and a grim expression on his usually friendly face.

"What's next, Ed?"

Imowelo brightened. "You fixed Tammy."

Ford grimaced. "I did not. Nor did Nilo. We tried. It's a miracle this town wasn't blown away on the last dust storm."

Imowelo spread his arms out. "I know what you're saying. If it's not our fabled Town Manager, it's a rover, or the HVAC down on the Farm. As soon as we patch anything, something else breaks down. You'll get used to it, Brother — you're in Cratertown."

▼

Out in the streets, Thuvia Lofgren popped out of a narrow passageway, looked around to be sure the coast was clear, then scampered across East Lateral, ran a block down Southeast Crossing, and ducked into the Township warehouse.

PODCAST HOST:

Hey out there. This is Thuvia, *The Real Maid of Mars,* reporting from the back streets of The Ark.

Today's topic — survival.

I used to live just off Interplanetary Highway, but now it's too dangerous. I'm on the run. Stealing food, holing up wherever I can.

Why, you ask?

Well, here among the Like Minded, mother and father must share the task of raising their children. It's an unbreakable rule.

Sadly for me, mother and father are not married, and they aren't even in a relationship. They were, though, for a little while.

That's right, you guessed it — *I'm pregnant.* Going on three months.

So far, the morning sickness crap you always read about is over with, so that's my big news.

Stick around and I'll keep you up to date. In six months or so, I'll let you know how the story ends.

18

CRAZY TAMMY didn't lock everything up." said Hoberman, half to himself. He was studying Township plans on his laptop. "Hey, Joe, I got something."

Ford looked up from the pile of helpdesk repair tickets he was sorting through. He bent over Hoberman's shoulder and peered at the screen.

"That damned telescope."

"You were out there."

"Oh yes."

Hoberman clicked on a button, and the screen shifted to reveal a list of telescope parts. He pointed at a circuit board hardened against radiation damage.

"I remember you told me it can talk."

"That's right, it can."

Hoberman spread his arms. "Well? I'm looking at a PP-64-80 voice module here on this page."

"So you are."

"So we remove the telescope's voice module and install it in the Town Hall. Give Tammy new pipes."

"Would that work?"

"Tammy chats through a PP-64. She's dash-fifty. The telescope's dash-eighty is designed to operate in hostile environments, but it should be software compatible."

Ford dialed a call on his handheld.

"Ed? It's Joe. I need a rover with a charge that will reach Boskovoy's telescope."

Pause.

"Make that today, basically now."

▼

At the last minute, when Ford and Hoberman were ready to board their bus, his apprentice was called away to an Active Deacon meeting.

Ford dialed Imowelo again.

"Ed — what's the protocol on rover activity? Nilo's unavailable. Is it okay if I go solo?"

Imowelo gave Ford the okay. Rover travel, Ford learned, was considered routine, providing space weather cooperated.

Ford checked the latest bulletins on his handheld. Quiet Sun, no flares, no mass ejections heading for Mars, so no cautions.

Ford waited patiently in the rover garage while pumps stored its air in a pair of huge rubber bladders. Soon the garage was in a near-vacuum. The exterior doors rolled open, and Ford rolled out onto the floor of the immense crater that cradled the human settlement.

After rolling northeast for four and a half kliks, the Flight Operations Center emerged out of the dusty haze that was a constant feature of the Martian atmosphere. Ford kept an eye out for the tracks left by his previous foray. And there they are! He tilted the rover's control stick left and headed due north.

Seven kliks later he cautiously worked the rover up a doubtful track onto a broad mesa. There he parked beside the telescope's concrete pillar. Looming above it, glittering in the sunlight and framed by the nearly black sky overhead, was the fragile telescope itself.

▼

Back in the Township, Nilo opened the door to a small office and entered a darkened room. A voice he knew well, the Counselor's, spoke softly.

"Welcome, Deacon Hoberman."

He felt around for a chair and sat down.

"Tell us what's going on with Brother Ford," came another voice, this one belonging to his fellow Active Deacon, Lycus Salazar.

Hoberman cleared his throat. "Not much," he said.

"What does he know? What has he found out?"

"Nothing. We're just working our butts off every day, repairing our screwed up systems."

"Some of our systems don't need an immediate repair, Nilo," declared a third voice, a vibrant and masculine baritone.

"Founder?"

"We don't use names here. Be watchful, be righteous in service to our sacred Independent Republic."

"Yes, sir. I mean, yes — whoever."

Twelve kliks to the northeast, on the mesa rising out of the crater floor, Ford lowered his suit's globular helmet over his head and tightened it down on the ring around his neck. Wearing the protective gear made him feel like a diver in one of those old treasure-hunting movies. Only no lead boots here, no treasure, no terrifying octopus to contend with. Just a tall ladder.

Ford pressed the transmit switch on the rover's radio. "Ford at the telescope, preparing to ascend," he reported.

The rover station wasn't routinely monitored by a human being, but if something went wrong, he hoped a concerned citizen would check. Sure, he sighed, and monkeys might fly.

He studied the ladder for a few minutes, working up his resolve.

"Fuck it, let's go."

He bounced out of the rover and clambered up the ladder as quickly as possible, before his ungovernable fear of heights could take over.

Inside the telescope's service package he identified the PP-64 unit and unplugged it.

"Sorry if this stalls your data stream, Zoran."

Then he was down the ladder and back in the safety of the rover. He repressurized the cabin. Off came the helmet. He checked his watch.

"Less than an hour."

He looked closely at his radiation tag.

"And I'm clean."

▼

Hoberman excused himself from his meeting and hiked across town to the Barsoomian Bakery. The morning crush had abated, and in order to keep out of sight, he took up a position washing dishes and restocking the pastry shelves.

He had reason to hope that Lofgren would eventually appear, and after the soiled dishes were all clean, she actually did.

"Hey, Thoo, in here."

He guided her into the tiny kitchenette behind the counter. Her eyes darted here and there, nervously scanning for trouble.

"Nilo! Thanks for meeting me."

"I got your text. What do you think you're doing?"

"Hiding."

"I listened to your podcast, so I know you're pregnant. *Pregnant!* And you're how old? Twelve?" He brought a hand up to his face, mocking a slap of astonishment. "Worse, I'm pretty sure I know who the father might be."

"It's certainly not you," she sniffed.

"How could it be? We never . . ."

"No, we didn't."

"Look, Zoran is an older guy, but he's not a monster. You look terrible. Why the drama?"

Lofgren sat herself down on the counter. She picked up a scone and nibbled on it.

"I'm not going to marry Zoran, Nilo. He's not going to talk me into it, and you and your precious Active Deacons are not going to force me."

She grabbed an apple and started gnawing.

"Also — it's a project. You know, desperate kid, against all odds, blah blah blah. Great episodes for my work."

"Good Christ, you are insane."

"I was hoping you could help me, star in my next show."

"I will do whatever I can. Need a bed? You could stay at my place, or . . . what's wrong with the women's dorm?"

"Your place sounds wonderful."

"You could take a shower. You need one."

"I dunno. It's great to be grimy."

"Anything you say, as long as you promise that I will *not* be the star of your next show. Or any future shows while you're farting around like this."

"Don't worry, I'll anonymize my benefactor."

"Thuvia — !?"

Her shouted name jarred them both. They looked around for someone to go with the voice, which belonged to Boskovoy, but the man was not yet in sight.

"Oh my God — he knows where I am."

Lofgren threw the apple into the sink, planted a quick kiss on Hoberman's cheek, and ran away into the tangle of Township corridors.

▼

Three kilometers away, Joe Ford was nearing the settlement when his rover suddenly lurched to his right.

"Oh shit."

He jostled the stick back and forth without effect. The vehicle slewed around in the sandy track and veered down a sharp incline into a shallow secondary crater. There it skidded sideways across the bottom and fetched up hard against the far rim, tilting over on two wheels.

"Oh no, no, no . . ."

A cloud of gravely dust particles blew up around the machine and fell back to the ground almost instantly in the very thin air.

Ford crouched down, waiting for his ride to roll over. But it remained at a forty-five degree angle, supported in place by the crater wall. Ford tried the controls. They were dead. He checked his oxygen gauge. Unless he took decisive action, pretty soon he was going to be dead too.

He searched the cabin for evidence of the rover's guidance computer without success. Then he remembered how Martian rovers were designed. Their smarts were all collected into a box that opened on their exterior surfaces for easy maintenance in the shop. And the door to the box on this rover was pressed against the crater rim by two tons of metal.

How far to The Ark? Three kliks? What time is it? Almost eighteen hours. Sunset pretty soon. He might be able to hike the distance, a matter of less than an hour, but once night set in, he would surely become very, very cold. Better get going.

He hooked his suit up to the rover's oxygen supply and filled the tank on his back. He donned his helmet and carefully stowed the telescope's PP-64 speech module in a shoulder bag.

Then he set out for a late afternoon stroll across the sandy soil of Mars.

Within a hundred yards he learned that being cold was not going to become an immediate problem. Instead, churning through the sand was hot work. His helmet threatened to fog over.

Worse, he realized that the ever-present haze concealed the outlines of his destination from view. And since Mars lacked a global magnetic field, he had no compass. He opened up the direction app on his handheld. Early explorers had thoughtfully placed positioning satellites in Mars orbit, but not many of them, and most had died long ago. At the moment, none of those still in working order were above the horizon.

"Where the fuck am I?"

Then, just short of despair, he noticed Phobos crossing overhead. The arc of the moon's travels high above Mars' equator gave him the sense of direction he needed and revealed that he was going the wrong way.

"Damn."

He turned southwest and trudged on, hoping in vain for a glimpse of the settlement's towers and antennas.

At five minute intervals he checked the phone service on his handheld. No signal.

He glanced at the long shadow he cast, saw it disappear as the sun fell behind the high western wall of Klickitat Crater.

Now, with twilight fading, he started to cool off. Within minutes the Martian temperature was far below zero on anyone's gauge. How far to go? Maybe another kilometer?

His handheld vibrated. He checked the signal strength and now saw three bars. He must be getting closer.

"Joe? Where are you?"

"Nilo?"

"Hey, old man, you're late. I got worried."

"Good for you. My rover gave up, so I'm hiking home, but I can't actually see the town."

"Okay. I'll light a strobe."

Ford came to a halt and surveyed the horizon.

"Show me that beacon."

A bone-chilling few minutes elapsed while he waited in place for Nilo's cue. Then a blue light flashed. On, off, on, off. It put Ford in mind of nineteenth century lighthouses, those quaint navigation aids for ships at sea. The sailors on those ships could never have imagined anyone navigating a frigid desert on this forbidding planet.

"Good Lord, I'm off by thirty degrees. But, hey, close enough."

He aimed at the light and stumbled toward it, one foot in front of the other, timing his steps to match the rhythm of the flashes. At last he saw floodlights coming into view on the water towers, the rover portal, and the Township's airlocks. His heart swelled to see them. They looked warm and inviting, almost like home.

19

GOOD MORNING, Brother Hoberman, how nice to see you." The decorous voice floated out of the Town Hall's main screen from the image of a matronly woman. Neither voice nor image belonged to any real human being, however. Instead, the sights and sounds were a double triumph of modern computing power.

"She's back, she talks!" exclaimed Hoberman.

"That's the Cycler's voice," said Ford, a little taken aback.

"Yeah. All the ships use PP-64s now. Once they were unique to really big data systems. Now even telescopes talk. Isn't that right, Tammy?"

"I have a very popular voice and a winning personality," she said. "Rated four-point-eight-five stars in fifty-two hundred reviews." She sounded petulant.

One of her lenses zoomed in for a closer look at the Earthman. "Your companion is unknown to me. Just a moment, please . . . checking ID's. Aha! — is this our new Immigrant, Citizen 503, one Joseph Ford?"

"That's me."

"Welcome."

"Glad to be here."

"You're listed as a maintenance engineer."

"That's right."

"I have several printers that need immediate attention."

"I'll bet you do, and we'll get to them, but first," — he consulted his handheld — "we need you to upload the print code for our low-power PP-020-M CPU and snap-in daughterboard to 3-D fabricator, um, looks like the ID is . . . Tars Tarkas."

"Tars Tarkas is offline and needs immediate attention. Will Kantos Kan work for you?"

The two humans looked at each other.

"Sure, if we can find it."

"Uploading . . . uploading . . . and there you go, upload complete."

"Thank you, Tammy."

"A pleasure, Gentlemen."

Ford shifted his weight around. "Wait a minute. We also need PP-64 replacements. And for that, please upload the fab code to our level two printer — hmm — Zodanga?"

"PP-64 code is locked. Current users are not authorized to print PP-64 CPUs without a password. Do you have that password?"

Ford frowned. "Got the word, Nilo?"

"Never heard of it."

"Fuck," said Ford.

"Invalid password. Such language."

Hoberman made a guess that the chip fabricator was located within the Town Hall behind locked doors. Tapping his combination on the lock opened the doors, and, sure enough, just past the server rack was another door, and beyond that a refrigerator-sized metal box with reservoirs of hard-to-identify fluids sitting on top; the machine they were looking for.

"How many parts do we want?" asked Hoberman.

"More than we need, for sure. Let's make a couple dozen."

Fabricating complex electronic parts in a 3-D printer was slow work. Hoberman stared at the little display screen while each copy of a PP-020-M CPU was meticulously created.

Now Fabricating PP-020-M CPU
Print 1 Substrate complete

Print 2 Trace Layer 1 complete
Print 3 Gate Layer complete
Print 4 Trace Layer 2 complete
Print 5 Package complete
Print 6 Daughterboard complete
PP-020-M CPU fabrication complete

When each part was finished, it dropped into a slot on the printer's front panel. Hoberman handed it off to Ford and reset the fabricator to turn out the next one. He was soon very bored.

Ford applied leads from his multiprobe to test each chip.

"All good so far," he announced. A glance at Hoberman, slumped in a chair and staring at something on his handheld, told Ford that his apprentice was not engaged with the task at hand.

"Look alive there, Nilo."

"I am alive. All ready to press another button. Love to press these things. I am a button-pressing ninja."

Ford chuckled.

"Forget about pressing Thuvia's buttons for a few minutes and tell me what you think of the Like-Minded way of operating. No government, loyalty pledges, personal restrictions?"

Hoberman sat up straight while he considered the question.

"I don't know what to think, but I'm careful, because I'm a designated Active Deacon, one of the Friends, and the wrong move can lead to trouble."

Ford nodded to show his sympathy.

"Are there dissidents? Citizens who might like to see some changes?"

Hoberman's face lost its color. "Maybe. But if so, I don't know them. Don't know anyone like that."

"What about my rover? Imowelo says the nav chip, a PP-020 like the ones we're making here today, blew up. Failed? Or, maybe one of your Deacon pals doesn't like me."

Hoberman almost laughed. "Well, the Friends have you pegged as a loose cannon, but I don't think anyone wants to kill you."

Ford shrugged to retreat from the idea.

"Okay. Eyes wide, though, you know?"

▼

Late in the afternoon, Ford found time to present himself to Dr. Rooney with new printer hardware and three new cartridges of printer ink.

"Hey, Doc. Printer maintenance," he announced, brandishing a newly fabricated computer chip nicely mounted on a little green circuit board. "Your ticket came up."

"Well, hello, there. I thought you'd forgotten all about me," said the doctor with a broad smile.

"Sorry for the delay. We only figured out how to make the part you need earlier today."

Rooney opened the document cabinet and dragged her printer out into the open. Ford pulled the old circuit board and installed the new one in its place, meticulously reconnecting the printer's wiring to the proper terminals.

"So far so good."

He pressed a button to turn it on. The machine's display screen lit up, and it worked through a series of warmup exercises, running the print head back and forth, spinning the paper advance rollers.

"Look at that," murmured Rooney. "Harvey is breathing."

"Harvey?"

"A giant rabbit in a very old movie. Now my pet printer."

"Really? You must be starved for companionship."

Ford extracted the machine's dried-up ink cartridges and snapped the new ones into place on the print head.

"Now comes the moment of truth," said Ford. "Will this thing print a test page?"

"Fingers crossed."

"Well, it's your printer, so you do the honors," — he pointed to a button on the display screen — "Tap your finger."

"Do I dare?"

"It may not work, but it won't blow up."

All right, here goes."

She tapped the screen, and a sheet of paper covered with statistics and little calibration marks in three different colors rolled into the output tray.

Ford and Rooney triumphantly bumped elbows.

"Ta-da!" she exclaimed. "Harvey lives! I'm so excited I could kiss you."

Ford braced himself for something he just now realized he was hoping for and actually expected. "Okay," he said.

Rooney threw her arms around his neck and crushed her lips against his. The revelation of their desires hit them both like an electric shock. Their tongues met. Ford cupped his hands under her bottom and lifted her off the floor. They whirled around in a dizzy embrace.

"Wait, wait a minute," she whispered, breathlessly disentangling herself. She strode to her office door and locked it.

"Office hours are over."

Ford picked her up, an easy feat in Mars' gravity, and carried her into the infirmary ward. "Care which bed?"

"Nope."

He dropped her on the nearest hospital bed and lowered himself down beside her. She unbuttoned his shirt. He yanked her blouse off and undid her bra. Soon their clothes were all over the floor.

She reached down and touched his crotch. He nuzzled her

breasts and rolled onto her. She turned over, threw a knee across his hip and sat on him. They were both breathing hard.

▼

When they came up for air an hour later, they looked at each other and laughed.

"What was *that?*" he wheezed.

"Two goats with big horns — that's my diagnosis."

"Wow," he said. He kissed her and nibbled on one of her earlobes. "Now I'm hungry. Let's go eat."

"I'm not sure that's a good idea. The gossip mill runs night and day around here."

"So what? People will find out anyway in this tiny town. We can supply some grist for their mill."

Ford heard Rooney's printer clicking and humming while he put on his clothes.

On their way out the door he noticed several sheets of paper in the output tray. He picked them up.

"What is this?"

Rooney peeked over his shoulder. "Well, I'll be damned. P.L.'s manifesto. I guess we wore the printer out before all the copies came through."

LIKE-MINDED CITIZENS *!*

The Ark is sinking — The system is corrupt
- Demand an end to religious tyranny
- Demand the right to vote
- Demand the rule of law

To repair our lives, we must institute a Government
If you agree, petition the Friends and the Founder

LET YOUR VOICE BE HEARD

"You knew."

"Of course I did. PL wasn't the only one who hates the system."

Ford rubbed his chin. "Okay, we printed the handbill. What about an autopsy report on P.L.'s death? Let's print that."

"All my documents are stored online with the Town Manager."

"Yeah, and you have medical authority over those documents. Let's see what you can do."

Rooney scowled. "Why dredge this stuff up? His air ran out."

"Right, but I want details. That's where devils hide."

Rooney shrugged and opened up her laptop. A brief tour through the Town Manager file system brought her up short. She pointed to an alert that appeared on her screen:

ARCHIVED MEDICAL FILES ARE LOCKED
FOR PATIENT CONFIDENTIALITY

Ford stared at the text. "Even for you, Doc?"

"Apparently so . . . even for me."

20

THE TOWN MANAGER was adamant. "Medical records are locked except for review by the owner."

"The owner is P.L. Scott. He wants to see them, but, uh-oh, he's dead," said Ford. He was sitting in the Town Hall facing a screen where The Ark's main computer was presenting itself as a stern grey-haired librarian.

"I'm so sorry. My thoughts are with his survivors."

"That's cute, Tammy. Your thoughts. Wow."

He wondered what joker had decided on the cliché graphics when the Town Manager software was installed back in The Ark's early days.

"I need an override. How do I proceed?"

"Higher authority."

"I can't call on God Almighty, Tam. How about this: you ever hear of the Planetary Settlement Agency?"

"Sounds like Earth business."

"Oh it is. I'm authorized by that entity to investigate irregularities in Ark governance. I'm an agent of the PSA. It's official. So, open up, please."

Tammy adjusted her glasses. She gave Ford an icy stare.

"We are no longer a colony, Brother Ford. We are The Independent Republic of Mars, and I cannot open medical records except for review by the owner."

"You said that already."

"I'll say it again — "

" — No, no, never mind. You are one tough chick, know that?"

Tammy scowled and screwed up her lips.

"Thank you, Brother Ford."

Ford leaned down to the backpack sitting between his feet and extracted the small meteorite he and Hoberman found in the West Side Auxiliary.

"Ready for a different job? I have here the meteorite that appears to be responsible for P.L. Scott's death. I want to record it in your database."

All of a sudden Tammy was wearing a white lab coat, white hair covering, and a pair of white gloves.

"Let me see."

Ford held the meteorite up and turned it back and forth.

"Hold object on its ends please and rotate again."

Ford repositioned his grip to be sure Tammy got the entire surface mapped.

"Details?"

Ford looked at his handheld notes. "Dimensions are — length, seventeen centimeters; width, thirteen centimeters; height, fifteen centimeters; weight approximately one hundred ninety grams."

A virtual reproduction of the stone magically appeared in Tammy's hands. She tipped her glasses down and gave it a close examination.

"Excuse me, Brother Ford, but this specimen appears to match Library catalogue item M-972-45-3H."

"Beg pardon?"

"It appears this meteor — or another one almost exactly like it — fell nine years ago."

"Mars years?"

"Yes. Seventeen Earth years."

▼

Ford had never seen a library quite like the one belonging to The Ark. No book shelves — no paper — just computer terminals and keyboards and glowing displays. Presumably they contained an immense number of volumes of every kind, but all in digital form. Ford passed them by.

In a room angling off the main area was a hallway lined with drawers stacked in rows. The meteorite collection occupied stacks 970 through 972. The meteorite that interested Ford was in drawer 45-H.

He opened the drawer. Item M-972-45-2H on the left was a stony chondrite that weighed more than half a kilogram. M-972-45-4H on the right was almost pure iron, the most common meteorite on Mars' surface, as easily collected by those venturing outside as seashells on an Earthly beach.

M-972-45-3H in the middle was a rounded nest lined with cotton wool. The label was clear and unambiguous. The item itself, however, was missing.

Ford delicately placed his meteorite in the empty nest. It fit perfectly.

"Ahhh . . ."

▼

In a darkened room, men were talking. One of them voiced an unwelcome development.

"You gave the stone to Brother Ford?"

"Yeah, I should have been more careful."

"Don't beat yourself up. He has no idea."

"Maybe not. Don't count on it."

"What does it prove if he finds out? Nothing, that's what."

An older voice inserted itself to manage the discussion.

"Let's not obsess. We have another problem — marijuana."

"That's right," said a younger voice. "I caught a whiff in Southwest Alley Four."

"Okay, where's it growing? The Farm?"

"Where else?"

"Hesperia would never allow anything like that," declared a resonant baritone.

"Then it's been concealed. We should monitor power usage. Someone might be running grow lights all night long."

"Then we locate the crop and burn it."

"Whoever is behind this betrayal of our values should have an accident," said the older voice.

"How serious?"

" Make sure he'll recover," said the baritone.

STEP **THREE**

21

Come this way."

Dana Rooney took Joe Ford's hand in hers and led him down an alley, through an airlock, across Interplanetary Highway, and west through a narrow HVAC Tunnel.

"Why the back streets?" asked Ford, amused by her caution.

"Well, we're out and about, but we don't have to *parade* ourselves."

"You're funny," he said. "Bold as brass, yet a daughter of modesty. Who was it? Mom? Dad?"

Rooney's eyes flashed. "Mom was very strict. Dad did not give a shit. Guess who I take after."

She came to a stop in front of an apartment in the West Residence District and gestured toward the entrance.

"Here we are." She touched the lock sensor with her handheld and pushed the door open.

Ford looked around. The place was twice the size of Dale's, where he had spent an uncomfortable sojourn. The little cooking surface had three burners instead of two. The refrigerator was as tall as he was.

"In there, bathroom," — she pointed — " and here, bedroom."

Ford stared at the bed. It was pure luxury by Mars standards.

"It's a double. But you're not married."

"You noticed. I was assigned the unit that belonged to a sweet old couple who passed away."

"I get it, make the new doctor feel welcome."

"I've got valuable skills."

"Oh yes."

He pulled her close and began unbuttoning her blouse. She

returned the favor and gave him a shove. He toppled — lightly — onto the bed and drew her down beside him for a kiss. They rolled toward each other.

▼

"I know why your marriage failed," said Rooney.

They were lying together in a warm embrace, half asleep, exhausted by their passionate exertions.

"Is that so?" murmured Ford.

"The tradition here is rain on the wedding day."

"Hmm, a blessing we were denied."

"Yes, fate intervened. Now it's us."

Ford grinned. "Here's to us." He rubbed his nose against hers.

Rooney pulled herself free and sat up.

"By the way — a new doctor will arrive on the next shuttle. My indentured servant time will be up, my medical education will be paid for, and I will be returning to Big Blue, debt-free."

Ford ran a finger along her thigh. He frowned.

"This is news. And we're just getting to know each other."

Rooney bent over him. "No lies, right?"

"I'm all for truth, babe."

She pushed her hair away from her face. "I love the bright lights and big cities. And here we have . . . Cratertown. Ugh."

"Not exactly Times Square," conceded Ford. Where is she taking this, he wondered.

"There is a solution to the problem." — she gazed at Ford with measuring eyes — *"come with me.* You're not really meant to be here either."

Ah, so that's it.

"Le me think. You're right, I'm a fish out of water — but I have to solve a crime."

"You've got a month."

22

OUT ON THE FARM, Hesperia Dale spent a long afternoon grafting hamburger bush cuttings onto reliable rootstock stems. She finished up by planting sixty-four of them in an open patch of Martian soil she had worked hard to amend with dry human manure and ammonia. She was dirty and sweaty, but she looked upon her labors with satisfaction.

She stripped off her gloves and her knee pads and rewarded herself with a leisurely stroll through the Farm's orchards, wending her way in between the apples and pears, the mangoes and peaches, humming a tune. As she walked along under the leafy canopy she felt her spirits soar. She liked to imagine that the landscape resembled the national parks on Earth she had read about. And yet, she didn't try to hide from herself the suspicion that the bleak sameness of Mars is what produced her hunger for greenery. And perhaps, she told herself, her well-known standoffish demeanor.

The trees opened up onto rows of fruits and vegetables. Half concealed Among the tall tomato cages, heavy with bright red fruit, she noticed a garland of blazing white lights.

"What the hell . . ."

She squeezed between the vines and stared at a half dozen plants of a different kind planted in between rows. Drip irrigators were piped in to water them. A long extension cord leading away to a utility shed powered the lights.

She fingered the spiky lobes of one of the leaves, noted a pungent odor.

"What am I looking at?"

She peered around the area, hoping that the gardener who did the planting might come and explain, but the Farm seemed empty of other human beings. She rubbed her chin and wrinkled her nose. Then she picked up her handheld and made a call.

"Joe? It's Hesperia. Hey, I'm on the Farm, looking at some unfamiliar plants and some gizmos set up to cultivate them. Lights, irrigation lines. I have never seen anything like them. Hate to bother you, but want to help me figure them out?"

▼

Ford took the call while he was working on the ice cream dispenser in the Main Street Food Hall. He was surprised to hear from his estranged wife.

"What do I know about plants, Hesper? Nothing."

"I know, we're not friends, but you're from Earth. Pretty sure that's where these plants come from. Unauthorized plantings are forbidden, so they must have value, and I don't dare remove them unless I've got backup."

"You're scared."

She bobbed her head up and down. "I've got a secret garden here. It's spooky, and trouble cannot be far away."

Ford blew out a sigh. "All right. You're a hike, so hang in there."

▼

It took Ford fifteen minutes to cover the distance between the Food Hall and the Farm. Dale met him at the main airlock and spent ten more minutes guiding him across the Farm's ample acreage to the suspect plants growing among the beans and tomatoes.

"What do you think?"

Ford didn't have to work hard to make an ID. "It's Mary Jane, Hesper. Oh-ho, you're a pothead."

"Cannabis. I thought so, but I've only seen pictures in books."

"Funny, all the secrecy," said Ford. "This stuff is perfectly legal back on Earth."

"But not here among the Like Minded."

"No."

Dale tugged on a stem. She bit her lip.

"I'm worried about Buster. What might happen to him."

Ford ran a hand through his hair. "You should be. I've seen how this works."

Ford began tearing out the plants. Dale traced the irrigation lines back to their water source, disconnected them, and rolled them up. She made a move to rip out the lights as well, but Ford shot out a hand to stop her.

"Dark soon," he said. "The lights are beacons. Let's see what kind of bugs they attract."

They retreated behind a screen of bean trellises and sat down to await events.

Five minutes went by. Dale shifted her weight around. "What are we doing? Buster might not show up for days."

"The chance we take."

They were silent for a while, content to watch daylight fade from the translucent roof.

Ford zipped up his jacket. "Will it get cold now?"

"No, the heaters will kick in."

And a moment later an audible *whoosh* told them the heaters were in good working order. Ford pointed into the distance.

"There, I hear the fans — what if there's a malfunction?"

Dale shrugged. "Never on my watch. Some of the fruit would die, of course. But we have a pretty complete seed base stored in our ag vault. We wouldn't starve."

"That's a relief. Everything else is falling apart."

An awkward silence returned. Ford pawed the loose soil with a plant stake. "Tell me about Like-Minded names. Ismenius, Nilosyrtis . . . and you, *Hesperia*. They're flowery. Unusual."

Hesperia smiled. "All recycled from planetary features on old maps. Maps made by astronomers who were imagining things. And Edgar Rice Burroughs, too, of course."

"Of course . . . Thuvia, *Maid of Mars*. I read the book."

"Pulp fiction, that." Dale studied the Earthman, curious about how well he was adapting to Township life. "Reality not what you expected when you signed up, I take it."

Ford grimaced. "Well, I had high hopes . . . tempered now by everyday life, that's true. But things are improving."

"You think so?"

"Yeah — fits and starts. Fits and starts."

Dale nodded. She let a long minute pass, then took a deep breath and decided to press an inquiry, confirm a rumor.

"So, Brother Ford — here's another flowery name — *Eridania*. How are things going with Dr. Rooney?"

Ford froze. He stared at Dale, surprised by her interest. Okay, he thought, if she wants to know . . .

"Kind of personal that question, yeah? But hey — we're living together, in her unit. Big enough for two."

Dale raised a knee and clasped her hands around it. She smiled. "So the stories are true. You in love with her?"

Ford's face reddened. "For God's sake, Hesper."

"Well, are you . . ?"

He shook his head. "Truth is, it's hard to tell. We're all over each other. But there's a problem. She's heading back to Big Blue, wants me to come with her."

Dale rocked back and forth, unsettled by the news. "Why is that a problem?"

"I'm not sure I want to go back."

Dale absorbed Ford's explanation in silence. She lifted a warning finger. "Hear that?" she whispered.

Ford nodded.

Someone was shuffling toward them through the crops, scraping up against the bushes.

"What in the world?" came a voice from the other side of the bean trellis.

Ford and Dale stood up.

"Buster? That you?"

Buster Mayfield took a big step backward.

"Jesus Christ," he said.

Dale's brow was creased by a deep frown. "Buster, how could you do it?"

Mayfield shrugged a guilty shrug.

Dale's face turned white with anger. "It's a betrayal — to me, to The Ark. My God."

Mayfield pushed his hands deep into his pockets. "I know," he said.

"Where did you get the seeds?"

Mayfield shuffled his feet around. "Came with that last batch of potato starters. Folks are looking for a little recreation, so I said okay."

Dale waved him away. "Jesus, you're the most Like-Minded person on Mars. Have you lost all judgment? Get out of here, go home. We'll take care of this."

Mayfield scratched his head.

"I can't go anywhere. The Deacons said to meet them on the Farm, at the, um, scene. They're coming along, be here soon."

Ford stirred. "They know about this?"

"Guy was smoking where he shouldn't have. One of the Deacons smelled it. I'm here for my beating."

Ford and Dale traded glances. "No one is going to beat you up, Buster."

"I know I crossed the line. I'm ready. It's expected."

Ford pulled his custom multiprobe from his work belt and threw a switch. Lights flickered on the probe. He threw another switch. The thing emitted a thin squeal as it powered up. He threw a third switch. A small electric charge danced across the probe's test points.

"Ain't going to happen, you understand?"

Ford looked around, clocked the nearby utility shed. He gestured toward it.

"Hesper and I will be right over there when the goons arrive. Meanwhile, you stand guard over these lights."

"You mean I'm the bait?"

"That you are, my friend."

"It's bad practice to mess with the Deacons, Joe."

"You let me worry about that."

Ten minutes elapsed while Ford and Dale huddled in the utility shed keeping a close eye on Mayfield, who stood near the garland of grow-lights, stiff as a statue.

Pretty soon the beams of flashlights skittered over the trees and shrubs. They fastened on Mayfield, picking up beads of sweat on his dark face.

Ford recognized Lycus Salazar.

"Good evening Brother Mayfield," said Salazar. "Active Deacons at your service."

Coming up behind him was someone he didn't recognize.

"That's Trivium Quinn," whispered Dale.

Salazar picked up the shovel Ford had been using to tear out the plants. He smacked the blade against a fist.

Mayfield's knees gave away, and he sank to the ground.

Now edging into the light came a third young man looking scared and queasy.

Ford let out a howl and charged out of the utility shed.

"Nilo Hoberman — what in God's name are you doing here?"

Hoberman stopped short, but said nothing.

Salazar turned toward Ford. He lifted the shovel, prepared to strike. "Watch yourself, Brother Ford. This is Deacon business. You'd best be on your way to supper or some such." He aimed an open palm at Dale, who was now advancing into the little group. "You too, Sister."

Ford puffed out his cheeks. "You're the ones going home. You believe in Like-Minded ideals? Then you better conform. Understand me?"

"Give me that," said Quinn, taking the shovel from Salazar. "Who is this guy thinks he can scare us?"

"Be my guest," said Salazar, nodding toward the farmer.

Quinn made a move toward Mayfield. Ford stood in his way. Quinn raised the shovel to strike. Ford shoved his multiprobe into Quinn's midsection and pressed a button.

zzapp

Quinn's arms went wide. He toppled backward and hit the ground hard. The shovel flew way into the bushes.

Salazar growled something unintelligible and took a swing at the Earthman. Ford ducked inside the punch, jammed the multiprobe against Salazar's ribs and let loose another charge.

zzapp

Salazar spun around and collapsed.

Nilo Hoberman's eyes were as wide as dinner plates. He could not believe what he was watching.

"Nilo?"

Hoberman blinked. "You . . . you hit a *Deacon.*"

Ford brandished his probe. "There's more where that came from. You should be ashamed of yourself."

Hoberman swallowed hard. "I am," he said.

"Then get out of here."

Dale jammed fists on her hips. "Spread the word. The Deacon's reign of terror is over."

Ford was slow to realize what he had just accomplished. Now he grinned. "Got that, Nilo? What the lady said."

▼

Later, when Mayfield and his would-be attackers had also been sent on their way, Dale gathered up the grow-lights and unplugged them. In the sudden darkness Phobos could be seen riding high above the Farm's translucent roof.

Dale pointed. "Look, there's Deimos too."

Ford gave the smaller moon a quick glance while he discharged his multiprobe and reattached it to his work belt.

"Fear and Panic," he said.

Dale looked upon the Earthman with something like new-found respect. She draped her arms over his shoulders.

"That was pretty cool what you did, Tarzan," she said.

He chuckled. "I might get into trouble over this."

"Oh yes, you will. The Deacons are not going away."

She gave him a quick hug, a kiss on the cheek, and then, embarrassed, backed away.

"I'm supposed to keep an eye on you, tell Ismenius and the Founder what you're up to. Now I've got something to report."

"Well, Hesper, make me look good."

She reached for his hand. They shook.

"Take care of yourself, Joe. Remember where you are."

"Yeah . . . Cratertown."

23

W HEN JOE FORD woke up, Dana Rooney was already dressed and out of their unit. He vaguely remembered a kiss and tousled hair.

Following his one-minute shower, he trudged out along West Residence and dodged through one of the HVAC corridors to the Food Hall, where coffee and a donut made time to think.

He wasn't surprised to see Nilo Hoberman striding across the floor in his direction.

Hoberman rounded up a Martian Moon and coffee of his own. He hesitated to sit down with Ford.

"Morning, old man," he said.

Ford gestured toward an empty seat.

Hoberman parked himself. They sipped their coffee in silence for a while.

"I'm supposed to find you and give you a message from the Friends," said Hoberman at length. He could barely get the words out.

Ford held up a hand. "Of course you are. To make it easy for you, give the Friends a message from me instead."

Hoberman chewed timidly on his pastry, raised his eyebrows.

"It starts with a question: who planted the meteorite in the West Side Auxiliary where P.L. Scott was found?"

Hoberman turned pale. "Planted? No one, that's crazy."

Ford stared hard at his apprentice.

"I know it was planted, Nilo. When I checked it into the Township collection, Tammy told me it fell nine years ago. I found an empty slot in the Library — M-972-3H. Whaddaya know? Perfect fit."

A trickle of perspiration appeared on Hoberman's forehead.

"So, Brother Nilo, recent addition to the Active Deacon ranks — no lies."

Hoberman nodded.

"What do you suppose the fraudulent evidence tells us?"

Hoberman considered the question.

"Something is wrong with P.L.'s death, I guess."

"You're telling me. It was no accident. So, again — who planted the stone?"

Hoberman's eyes rolled around, looking desperately for a way to escape.

"I don't know who," he said at last. "No idea."

Ford suppressed the anger rising in his throat.

"Ever hear the expression, *lie down with dogs, wake up with fleas?*"

Hoberman looked puzzled. He shook his head.

"What's that mean?"

"You're in bed with thugs, Nilo. Watch out you don't turn into one of them."

▼

Later in the morning, Ford climbed a ladder running inside the East End Radio Antenna tower. He was there to inspect the receiver, for which Ed Imowelo had prepared a Helpdesk ticket. Something intermittent was degrading reception.

Ford cared little about the signal quality, however. The location afforded a secure opportunity to make a private transmission of his own to Earth's Planetary Settlement Agency.

He connected the leads of his multiprobe to the power lines of the Township radio, inserted his tiny transducer into one ear, and flicked a switch.

An interplanetary message was waiting for him, floating in an ocean of electromagnetic noise.

> *Hello, Blue Eyes. Squawk channel six-four-niner and*
> *make your report. Two-way delay is three-three minutes*
> *as of oh-nine-twenty-one.*

Ford peered through a window in the tower wall. He could see
the bottom third of the main antenna and beyond it, barely visible
though pink haze, the distant rim of Klickitat Crater, his present
and lonely position. He imagined the weather in Santa Monica,
California, where any call he made would likely be received. Sun,
mild temperatures, rolling surf on the Pacific Ocean. He sighed,
and pressed six, four, nine on his multiprobe keypad.

> *BlueTalk, agent Ford here on the high side. Opposition*
> *to my presence is emerging in the form of veiled threats.*
> *Accordingly, I hereby invoke Protocol Two. I say again,*
> *Protocol Two. Beginning now, I will transmit proof-of-*
> *life on a five-day rotation, using my established*
> *credentials — credentials which I certify are not known*
> *to anyone else in the Settlement.*

He released the transmit button and took a breath. Then he
added a note:

> *If I fail to report, be prepared to shuttle a squad to The*
> *Ark. The good citizens here will need your help, and I*
> *might be dead.*

24

COUNSELOR POMERANCE sat in his tiny office and stared at the text of a diplomatic message that had just arrived in his printer. It bore the seals and identifying hallmarks of the Planetary Settlement Agency, the government group on Earth that had once ruled over The Ark. The contents of the message disturbed him. He reached for his handheld to call Joseph Ford, but was interrupted by the man himself.

"May I come in?"

Pomerance gestured him inside.

"I think you better. I just received a message from our former masters. It concerns you."

Ford sat himself down in Dale's prototype chair.

"Something like this?" he asked, rigging his multiprobe to play an incoming message of his own through the machine's tiny speaker.

> *Blue Eyes, considering the likelihood of murder in the Settlement, be assured we accept Protocol 2. We trust you will remain safe and await your regular transmissions.*

"Murder? Are you out of your mind!?" roared Pomerance. He leaped from his office chair and paced a circle around Joe Ford.

"I'm warned by the hated PSA to take whatever measures might become necessary to keep you safe. An illegal order, by the way, an undisguised threat to our sovereignty." He ran a hand through his dark hair. "As if anyone Like Minded would dream of harming you."

Ford chuckled. "Your Deacons don't seem to share your faith."

Pomerance brought himself to a halt. "The marijuana thing."

Ford nodded. "That's right, Counselor, I was attacked when I defended Brother Mayfield. I've seen your Deacons in action, how they enforce your rules, such as they are. I'm here to tell you their reign of terror is over. But now I have to worry about retribution."

Pomerance snorted. "Don't be silly. But murder? The matter was settled five months ago. What sadistic impulse possessed you to pry it open again? You're reaching far beyond yourself."

"Am I? The meteor that Nilo found might have caused the air leak that killed P.L. Scott — but it didn't. It was planted."

Pomerance tipped his head to stare at the Lord above. "That is absurd. Who would ever do such a thing?"

"Tammy flagged the stone as Library Item M-972-45-3H. It fell nine years ago and was collected at the time. You should be opening an investigation."

Pomerance was fuming. "As Counselor, in order to investigate a crime I would have to call for the appointment of a police officer. A police officer! Do you understand what that would mean? It would bring the formal powers of government down on our heads. Well, I'm not going to do it."

Ford leaned forward. "Then allow me. You can relax. But to prove my case I need Tammy's cooperation, I need passwords to pry open her logs."

"I don't know about any passwords. Everything's public."

"Well, no it isn't. Or, try this — somebody decided some items should *become* private. Somebody who didn't know how to actually erase incriminating records."

Pomerance sank back in his chair. He gazed at the newcomer, trying to gauge all the trouble the man was likely to cause. He rubbed his chin.

"Brother Ford — how do you suppose we survive, since we lack the political structures so dear to your Earthly friends? Do you think it's as simple as faith and prayer? Is that what you think of life in The Ark?"

"That's what we're told, in the training."

Pomerance was out of his chair again. "Of course, and it's true. But there's a subtle social pressure here too. Those who aren't truly Like Minded run the risk of becoming . . . unpopular."

Ford stood up to go. "I'll remember that. Something else to remember — the Puritans' stern ethic faded away under a different kind of social pressure."

The Counselor stepped around his desk and opened his office door. "There's never been a murder on Mars, Brother Ford, understand? Never in thirty years. Not one. Not a single violent crime of any description. We left that evil behind on Earth."

"Really," said Ford. "You're a good Christian . . . ever think about vanity? Original sin?"

He stepped into the hallway. An odd expression creasing the Counselor's face made him wait for a final word.

"Go ahead and make your ridiculous proof-of-life calls to Big Blue every five days," said Pomerance. "We don't need an army to keep the peace here."

He tapped a finger against his lips.

"And ask the Founder about passwords. He might know."

25

THE FOOD HALL was nearly empty of hungry patrons when Nilo Hoberman showed up for a takeout meal.

He collected oat milk, a plant-based chicken sandwich, two raspberry tarts, and coffee. He paid with his handheld and stuffed the food into a fiber carry bag.

On his way out he crossed paths with Zoran Boskovoy, who was looking for a late lunch. They waved to each other.

"Nilo, my friend."

"Brother Boskovoy."

Hoberman hurried down South Promenade through light afternoon foot traffic, meeting more people than he passed. After a hundred meters he began to sense someone following behind, pacing him. He glanced over his shoulder for confirmation, but couldn't really be sure. A hundred meters further along he abruptly ducked into the HVAC tunnel that provided a shortcut to the warehouse and the Township Media Studio.

Once well inside the narrow corridor he paused. Wait a minute, was that Boskovoy following him down the Promenade?

He pressed himself against the wall behind a service bin and trained his eyes on the square of brightly lit Promenade visible at the tunnel's entrance. A few seconds later a figure poked its head into view and squinted into the darkness. Hoberman felt himself stiffen.

The figure spent some time peering into the gloom, then withdrew and passed on down the Promenade.

Hoberman exhaled. It was definitely Boskovoy.

"Whoa, that guy . . ."

Following him, but looking for someone else, that he knew.

He quickstepped to the tunnel's far end and looked both ways for Boskovoy before venturing into the next brightly lit thoroughfare. After a careful survey failed to set off any new alarms, he zigzagged to his right and opened the doors to the warehouse. He was pretty sure he made the move without being detected. Then he crossed to the far side, opened another set of doors, bolted along East Central Boulevard for two blocks and let himself into the Rover Shop.

"Hey, Thuvia," he called out as he sauntered into the cluster of broken-down rovers.

Thuvia Lofgren leaned out of a narrow bay not far from P.L. Scott's ruined locker. She pulled off her headphones.

"Nilo? Over here."

Hoberman presented his carry bag.

"Your lunch, Sister Lofgren."

She opened up the bag, spotted the tart and wolfed it down, talking between bites.

"Think I'm safe here? It's cozy. I've got my handheld, I can record my podcasts. They'll sound kind of crummy, proving I'm on the run."

Nilo fidgeted with his coffee.

"Maybe you can then run my episodes back to the studio for me, send them out."

"I dunno, Thoo. I'm pretty sure Boskovoy was trailing me from the Food Hall. He's looking for you. I think he knows I'm your courier."

He reached into his carry bag for the second raspberry tart, which he had bought for himself. But Thuvia's eyes lit up when she saw it, so he handed it over.

Thuvia took a bite. Then she leaned close and gave Nilo an affectionate peck on his cheek.

"Sorry about hogging the dessert," she mumbled with her mouth full. "Starving."

"Pregnancy. Eating for a future person. I get it."

Thuvia finished the tart and started on her plant-based sandwich.

"If Zoran asked me, would I have to marry him? And, even worse, could he make me go with him when he cycles back to Earth?"

"Not sure how Like-Minded dogma applies to you."

"I thought you were studying this theological crap, Mr. Active Deacon."

"I was."

"Well, what *are* you doing?"

"Brother Ford — Joe — the Earthman — he and I are fixing things. Lot of work."

"Mmm."

"And you wouldn't believe the problems. Passwords for the Town Manager. We don't have them, and, man, do we need them."

"Passwords? Ooh, sounds like a puzzle."

"Yup. It's a good one."

PODCAST HOST:

Hello, friends of Thuvia, *The Real Maid of Mars.* Here I am improvising a post in the Cratertown rover repair shop. If I sound out of breath, I am — on the run again.

If the father of the child I'm carrying finds me, he could ask me to marry him. In Like-Minded culture I might have to accept. That cannot happen, so I'm no longer a citizen, I'm a wild animal, running, hiding, relying on scraps for my next meal, bedding down wherever I can find a hole.

I've seen Earth foxes in our virtual zoo. That's how I think of myself, slinking around, biting hard on any opportunity available to live my life.

Luckily, like some real foxes, I've got a human admirer. He brings me food, keeps his eyes peeled for the man who's hunting me. Can't tell you his name, 'cause he'll get in trouble, and he's the only thing between me and captivity.

Stay tuned. I might become a wolf — I've made friends with them in our zoo. Wouldn't that be something? Nobody messes with wolves, Like Minded or not.

26

W HO IS IT?"

Joe Ford was standing outside a residential door that barked out a challenge as he approached.

"Brother Ford," acknowledged the Earthman. He looked around. People were streaming back and forth along North Axis Promenade, oblivious to the arched doorway where Ford was waiting. They didn't seem to notice that the door was twice as wide as most, painted a subtle shade of green, and decorated with elaborate carvings inlaid with gold leaf. He thought it was a peculiar touch for a private residence in the otherwise egalitarian and workaday Martian settlement.

"Do you have an appointment?" inquired the door.

"Yes, courtesy of Counselor Pomerance."

"Please come in," said the door. It whipped aside into a hidden pocket, startling Ford.

He stepped through the doorway into a long and narrow corridor. Photographs on the walls depicted the early days of the settlement as it was being built. Prominently featured among the materials and machinery was a young and virile astronaut, grinning broadly to celebrate the immense achievement of carving out a place for human beings on a hostile world. Ford examined the images. He guessed that the astronaut was Hadley Timmerman, the famous settlement Founder, and the man he had just now come to see.

At the end of the hallway, the space opened up into a square atrium perhaps ten meters long and wide. In the middle of the square was a shallow pool. Water lilies were floating on the surface. Water bubbled from a fountain in the middle. Durable nandina bushes and a miniature weeping willow tree outlined its borders. Ford whistled. He was astonished by the opulence.

While he gazed at the water, half imagining he would soon see golden carp rising to the surface, an inner door opened. A young man emerged. He waved hello. Ford waved back.

"Lycus. Pardon my surprise. How are you today?"

"In good health, thank you. The Founder will join us shortly."

No sooner were the words out of Salazar's mouth than the door reopened and the ancient astronaut came scooting out into the open on his prosthetic wheelchair.

"Brother Ford!" boomed the Founder through his onboard speakers. "Welcome, welcome!"

Ford couldn't help himself and bowed his head to show respect. "Thanks for seeing me, sir."

"Not at all! Not at all!" The ancient one grinned. "You know Liko, I believe. He's here to watch over me."

Ford nodded. "We've met — more than once."

The Founder cocked his head. One pair of eyeglasses flipped up onto his forehead, and a pair of high powered goggles flipped down over his eyes. He squinted at Ford.

"No hard feelings after your recent encounter, I hope."

Ford tugged at an ear. How to respond? He decided to take a chance with the Founder's good will and be direct. "Well, sir" — he nodded toward Lycus — "with all respect to the Friends of the Like Minded, I don't believe citizens of The Ark should suffer physical abuse."

"Sometimes discipline is needed — " began Salazar. The Founder raised a hand to cut him off.

"Of course not, Brother Ford. It goes against our high ideals."

"My thought, sir," agreed Ford.

"And yet, social coherence is an absolute necessity. Sometimes the Friends stray."

"I hope my point of view will persuade you to, um, find *alternative methods,*" said Ford.

"Yes! Yes! I believe our newcomer has helped us see ourselves in a new light."

"Action in Harmony," said Ford.

"Harmony in Thought," added Salazar.

"And Thought in Action," finished Timmerman.

He spun his chair around to face Salazar. "Liko, my boy, let Brother Ford and myself have a few minutes, hmm?"

Salazar bowed his head and retreated into a side room.

Timmerman watched him depart. He sighed dramatically. "Small population, Brother. Labor in short supply, and we must take the men we can get, flawed as they may be. Lycus is attentive to my needs, and I have many."

"I understand," said Ford.

"Now then, what can I do for you?"

"Well sir, Nilo Hoberman and I are campaigning to fix everything that's gone wrong with The Ark. And in our work we need Tammy's cooperation."

'The Town Manager. Is that what they call the front end now?"

"That's right, sir. We're trying to repair some important devices — including Tam herself. So far, she doesn't respond readily to inquiries or commands. We're lucky she can still adjust the climate properly, make sure power is distributed."

Ford outlined the need to manufacture advanced computer chips, read important documents, check on repair records.

"We need passwords, sir. Passwords I'm told only you know."

As a gesture to indicate thinking, Timmerman slowly pivoted his wheelchair in an erratic full circle. Upon completing his contemplative turn, he pointed to a bench near the pool.

"Come, sit! Over here, wonderful spot!"

Ford let himself down on the bench.

"Your pool is beautiful."

Timmerman directed his wheelchair over beside him, maneuvering into place in stops and starts.

"Well," said the astronaut, "as they say in the army, *rank hath its privileges!* The Ark's good citizens have been very kind to me."

He adjusted the volume on his voice control to a more intimate level. "I hear you think we've had a murder. What do you say?"

Ford shifted his weight around. He felt like a lab animal being examined for some unknown disease.

"Not sure exactly what happened. I do suspect foul play in P.L. Scott's death."

"A murder! On Mars! In a group dedicated to the idea of perfect peace! Impossible!"

"Sorry, sir, but I need to pursue this. The evidence is solid."

The Founder expelled another loud sigh.

"Well, go ahead with your investigation. We'll call it *due diligence.* But be aware, if there are passwords, I don't remember them. At one hundred twenty-five years, I don't remember a lot of things."

Ford nodded. "Do my best."

The Founder was silent for a minute. Ford strained to see whether his eyes had closed behind the goggles he was wearing. But suddenly the old man sat up straight.

"You know," he said, "I wasn't Like-Minded when I led the team to start this habitat. But over the years the only recruits we could entice to immigrate were — you know the rest. Now it's The Ark, filled with visionary people. I've come around to their way of thinking — no government — trust in the Lord and humanity's good intentions."

He swiveled his wheelchair back and forth.

"I should be worried about you, but instead I'm worried about my controller. The damn thing is acting up. I don't want my chair to turn into a bucking bronco. Can you fix it?"

Ford raised a finger to salute the lucky opportunity.

"Maybe so."

He hefted his multiprobe, configured it into analytical mode by pressing a switch, and applied its sensors to the wheelchair's joystick. The probe noticed a power mismatch and a faulty connector. Ford delicately adjusted the battery output.

"I'm looking at a voltage mismatch. Somehow your chair's power sync got toggled to a slightly different state."

He jiggled the wire leading from the joystick to the wheelchair innards, tightening the connection.

"Try it now."

Timmerman used the controller to edge away from the pool. He bumped back and forth experimentally, then romped around his quarters, rolling, spinning, stopping and starting, as joyous and energetic as a kid.

"*Yippee-ki-yay!*" he boomed.

Ford watched him play. His mind was whirling.

CRATERTOWN   169

27

WHERE is that ridiculous woman hiding?

Zoran Boskovoy had already concluded that the best way to track down his pregnant ex-girlfriend was to lie in wait for her admirer and watch his movements.

Today, Nilo Hoberman headed obliquely for The Ark's Media Studio.

"Aha!" said Boskovoy to himself, who saw the young man's passage from the concealment of a nearby doorway.

He waited for Hoberman to reappear. After he was well out of the way heading back north on East Central, Boskovoy quietly slipped into the studio.

"Thuvia?" he called out. "Where are you? We've got a show to do. Let's get started."

Thuvia Lofgren was holed up in an out-of-the-way cubicle. Her headphones were on, and she was rocking to the beat of a recent Earth tune as she typed up the script for a new podcast. She didn't hear Boskovoy calling her name.

Boskovoy stood in the middle of the Studio's main stage listening for Lofgren's reply, or any evidence of her presence.

"Come on, Thuvia. Running away won't solve anything."

This time Lofgren heard a voice. She yanked off her headphones and leaned out of her cube.

"Thuvia!" Boskovoy's voice echoed through the Studio offices and stages.

Lofgren froze. Her heart was thumping. She felt limp.

"Hey, Kid. I know we're not really an item at the moment, but I would like to change that."

"Gotta move, lady," she mumbled and, using all her willpower, forced herself to take a step. Then another. And another. She bit her lip and tiptoed away from the voice.

Moving slowly and silently, Lofgren passed the Studio restroom and continued along the nearest hallway to the end, where she found a closed door. She opened it, crossed the threshold, closed it behind her, and hid herself on the other side. She was panting with anxiety.

Pretty soon she could hear footsteps coming her way.

"You're pregnant," observed Boskovoy, raising his voice enough to reach into every corner and crevice. "I know all about it, and I'm guessing I'm going to be Dad. Let's talk about the future, okay? Sound like a good idea?"

Lofgren was standing in the dark. She felt along the wall for an electrical switch and pressed it. A faint ceiling light bloomed halfway along a narrow corridor that opened into an attic filled with TV light stands, electrical cables, the walls of disassembled sets, prop desks, microphone booms, and a camera dolly. She worked her way through the clutter, momentarily envious of the superior TV tech she knew was in use on distant Earth.

Before she reached the far wall she heard a door bang open and Boskovoy shuffling toward her.

Oh man, gotta shake that guy.

She turned on a heel, scanning for any kind of hiding place, and saw none. But she did spot another door, this one half concealed behind a music synthesizer keyboard tilted up on one end. She carefully moved the keyboard aside, opened the door, and just as carefully repositioned it as she pirouetted inside, withdrew her hand, and closed the door behind her. As the latch clicked she heard the keyboard thump against the door's outer surface, restoring its disguise. She lit the flashlight on her handheld. Just above the latch she saw a second handle — *aha!* — a deadbolt.

She twisted the handle and threw the bolt.

"There," she whispered.

Outside, Boskovoy stood in the middle of the attic, lost in the forest of TV production gear.

"Okay, you're pretty clever, wherever you are. I'll let you go — for now. But we have to talk, my dear" — he turned away — "when you come to your senses."

Lofgren listened for his footsteps, trying to figure out if he had given up the chase or was setting a trap.

"Not going back out that way, Zoran — can't fool me today."

She turned around and felt her way down a dark corridor, looking and hoping for an alternative exit.

After thirty paces she came to a T-junction and more doors.

"Where am I, anyway?" she griped aloud.

She opened the nearest door and aimed her flashlight at the interior of a shallow closet. It's shelves were crammed with obsolete computer cables and modems and signal routers.

"Oh great. Here's Cratertown's antique store."

She tried the door to her left. Her flashlight caught the glint of steel tanks and a well-engineered tangle of pipes and ducts leading into deep gloom. She could hear pumps thrumming and liquids gurgling. Water purifiers? Air conditioning equipment? Sewage processing? She had no idea what she was looking at. Whatever it was, the brutal industrial appearance did not exactly promise an easy escape.

"Ugh. Belly of the whale," she muttered.

She looked around for any other possibilities. Off to her right the corridor angled around a tight corner and out of sight. She followed it to yet another door. Her flashlight beam illuminated a warning placard:

AUTHORIZED ACCESS ONLY

Lofgren gritted her teeth. "Well, shit, I authorize myself," she growled.

Not so easy. The door was locked. A daunting keypad barred her way. The digital obstacle might have deterred her, but she had never encountered anything like the kind of secrecy she was facing. It stirred her youthful curiosity and her determination.

By moving her flashlight beam obliquely around the keypad, she was able to detect that the 1, 2, 7, and 8, keys were lightly polished by use, but the others were not.

"Look at you," she said.

On her fifteenth try the combination 2-7-1-8 unlocked the door. She pushed it open and stepped into a storage room about the size of her residential bedroom. The walls were lined with shelves, and the shelves were filled with paper documents in folders and binders. She had found some sort of musty archive.

She pressed a switch near the door and the entire ceiling lit up. She ran a finger along the nearest shelf. The titles on the binders seemed antique:

HABITAT-1 ELECTRICAL CODE
HABITAT-1 AIRLOCK SECTIONS
HABITAT-1 TYPICAL SEAL DETAILS
HABITAT-1 PLANT INDEX

And, more intriguing:

HABITAT-1 OPERATIONS MANAGER

She remembered Nilo's frustration with computer passwords and recalled his devoted attention to her self-imposed predicament. A guilty shudder rippled down her spine. She pulled the binder off the shelf and opened it up.

"Passwords? What have we got here .. ?"

▼

Hoberman responded to Lofgren's urgent call and met her in the maintenance office he shared with Joe Ford.

"You sounded kind of breathless — everything okay? Baby kicking? What?"

Lofgren handed him the binder she found.

"Look at page seventeen."

Nilo opened the binder on his desk. Page seventeen listed a dozen cryptic text strings.

"Operations Manager" — Lofgren tapped a finger on the page header — "that's got to be the Town Manager, dear old Tammy. *And I found her passwords,*" she explained triumphantly.

"Most likely," allowed Hoberman, puzzling over the mysterious sequences . . .

QZ-237-FAv50

HAB1OM-admin

KEY-H1-users

ABC-$621-xyz

. . . and several more of similar nature, each twelve characters long. He saw no identification of any string with any particular function.

"Can't tell which ones will work, or what any of them might unlock. But . . . thanks. This is great stuff. Major discovery."

She nodded. "Forgotten archive — hidden away beyond the boiler room that spooked me— it's full of stuff like this. All on *paper,* can you imagine?"

She paused for effect.

"Do I get a kiss?"

28

HELLO, TAMMY ..."

Joe Ford and Nilo Hoberman were sitting at a pair of consoles in The Ark's Town Hall, facing the large display screen and the Town Manager avatar, who appeared in her librarian guise with bookshelves arrayed behind her. The binder Thuvia Lofgren found was open before them.

"Brother Ford, Brother Hoberman. How can I help you?"

Hoberman swallowed hard. He turned to Ford. "You sure about this? We're trespassing on Founder territory here."

Ford made a wry face. "Still the Active Deacon, I see. But you know better. Our inquiries are legit. Critical to system maintenance" — he thumped the binder — "and to my little investigation."

"Gentlemen?" frowned Tammy, "Why am I talking to you?"

Nilo cleared his throat.

"Okay, sorry . . . we want to see medical records for Percival Lowell Scott, please."

Tammy shook her virtual head. "Medical records are locked except for review by the owner."

"Command override, Tammy," ordered Ford.

Tammy tipped her reading glasses down over her nose. "Record release requires a password. Do you have it?"

"Which one do you think?" whispered Hoberman.

"Your guess is better than mine," replied Ford.

Hoberman pointed to one of them. "Start here?"

Ford nodded. Hoberman turned back to the Town Manager.

"Here you go, Tam — *HAB1OM-admin.*"

Tammy smiled. "Nice try. I'll give you two more attempts

before I end our conversation for security purposes."

"Christ, Nilo. *Think.*" whispered Ford.

Hoberman drummed his fingers on the password page.

"How about, *KEY-H1-users?*"

"Bravo! That will allow me to free up encrypted chip data, but not, I'm sorry to say, medical reports."

She pointed a finger.

"One more attempt."

Ford and Hoberman huddled over the password page.

"You know, we could do this again tomorrow, start over."

"I like today better."

"Yeah."

"What's the craziest string we've got?"

Hoberman tapped a line of text. "This one."

"Go. Go, go, go."

Hoberman drew a breath. "All right, Tammy old girl, here's what you want — saving the best for last — *QZ-237-FAv50 . . .*"

Tammy's library faded away. Suddenly she was standing in a hospital operating room wearing a hair net and surgical scrubs.

"Place a static storage device in Tray Six, please," she said.

"Damn, Nilo, got a drive?"

Hoberman dug around in his pockets and came up with a plastic disc the size of a button. He dropped it into Tray Six.

"Transferring P.L. Scott Autopsy Report, P.L. Scott dental records, P.L. Scott primary care examination history."

She shook a warning finger at her inquisitors.

"Acknowledge Restriction Protocol Med-21 — do not share this information with any person who lacks the necessary override credentials."

"Wouldn't dream of it, Tam," said Ford.

29

P.I. SCOTT'S medical information, openly sitting on Joe Ford's tiny storage disc, made Dr. Rooney uncomfortable.

"You want me to copy this?" she asked.

"That's right," he replied.

"You know you're talking privacy violation. I'm not authorized to see this stuff."

"Yup. You should never, ever do what I'm going to do."

He took the disc from Rooney and placed it on her laptop's reading tray. He pressed the CTRL and V keys.

Rooney folded her arms. "I thought you were Mr. Law and Order."

Ford chuckled. "We're in Cratertown. What law? What order?"

He picked up the disc and tucked it into a shirt pocket.

"Now you've got it. Let's print that autopsy report. Take a closer look at the man's way of shuffling off his mortal coil."

Rooney scowled. "You better hope I'm not held accountable. Unless you want the Deacons to beat me up."

Ford took Rooney in his arms and squeezed her tight. "Never, babe. Hit *print* for me."

Forty-five seconds later five pages dense with text and grainy photos spilled out of Rooney's newly-repaired printer.

"Asphyxiation," noted Rooney, "The official account."

Ford leafed through the pages.

"Mmm."

Rooney shook her head and waved airily to banish her suspicions. "Stand in a vacuum, given more than a very few seconds, and you die. We're on a planet with less than one percent of Earth's atmosphere, so why not?"

"I know" — he snapped a finger against a paragraph on page three — "why does he have dust in his lungs?"

Rooney had to think about that.

"Well, Mars is dusty. The Township is dusty. Maybe, when the air whooshed out of West Side Auxiliary, it stirred up the dust and P.L. sucked it in."

Ford squinted at her. "That's a reasonable theory — except, your good friend P.L. was not killed in that corridor. The meteor strike was a fake."

"You're sure? I'm not just a suspicious old nag?"

"Bet your beautiful ass."

▼

Knowing and proving were two different things, Ford reminded himself as he grimly vacuumed the synthetic floor covering in the West Side Auxiliary corridor.

He donned nitrile gloves to guard against contaminating important evidence, opened the vacuum dirt catcher, and poured its contents into a clear plastic bag. He peered at his catch. He had collected maybe ten grams of pebbles and dirt and hair and lint. At most.

"No dust," he said.

▼

In the early hours of the following day, Ford found himself stuck in his recurring dream. His body jerked and twisted as he tried to back away from the *carcelero,* and the man's small sharp object. Rooney grabbed his shoulders and shook him.

"Joe!"

"Mmm . . ."

He relaxed momentarily, but very soon he was back in jail. Now, he noticed, the small sharp object in the *carcelero's* hand was not a combat knife, not a dagger or stiletto, but the key to his cell.

The *carcelero* unlocked the cell door and threw it open.

"*¡Sal de aquí!*"

"What?"

"Get out of here! *Vuelve a Gringolandia, soldado. ¡Dile a tus camaradas que somos misericordiosos!*"

Ford saw his dream-self exit the jail and glide away among the derelict remnants of an enemy laser cannon and the ragged pine trees populating a cold mountain valley.

His eyes flew open and he sat upright. His heart was pounding. Rooney placed a hand on his chest.

"Jesus, Joe, calm down. You're okay. It's just a dream. You were dreaming."

Ford flopped back onto the bed.

"Scared me," he said.

It was Rooney's turn to sit up. She leaned over him.

"What scared you?"

Ford scratched his head. "I don't know. I was in the war, captured, awaiting execution, and instead of standing me up in front of a firing squad, the jailer guy opens my cell door and sets me free."

Rooney pondered this information.

"You remember the details. You've had this dream before?"

"Many times. A prisoner, ready to die, and I wake up alive."

"And you don't know what it means?"

"No. Wish I did."

Rooney repositioned herself on her side. She rubbed Ford's unshaven jaw. "Shall I tell you?"

Ford stared at her. "You take psych classes in med school?"

"That's a yes. So here it is — in your dream, your life is a lucky chance, a *gift.*"

"Okay, and thanks, I'll take it."

"Problem is, when life is a gift, you didn't shape it, you're not the author, so you don't *own it.*" She paused to let the idea sink in. "That's what scares you."

Ford was silent.

"Let's change the subject," he said at last.

Rooney rolled onto her back.

"Didn't mean to pry," she said.

Ford sat up and planted his feet on the floor. He ran a hand through his hair.

"There was absolutely no dust in the corridor where P.L.'s body was found. I checked. Now — why fake a meteor strike?"

"You got me, Detective."

"That's a rhetorical question — to cover up how P.L. really got killed. And where."

"But, Joe — dear — he did die of asphyxiation."

"Yes, and now we know there was dust in his lungs. Where did it come from?"

Rooney rotated out of bed and toddled off to the bathroom. While brushing her teeth a thought occurred.

"All right," she burbled through a mouth full of foam, "how's this? One of P.L.'s gigs was keeping the park clean. There's a lake in the park."

Ford bumped a fist against his head.

"Ahhh . . ."

▼

Ford stooped beside the majestic weeping willow tree at the edge of Central Park's decorative pond and scooped up a handful of mud, which he deposited in a plastic tub.

He struggled into an EVA suit, stepped into the main West Side Airlock, closed the interior door behind him, and when the light turned green, opened the outer hatch.

He trained his handheld on the mud-filled tub and began recording video.

As air escaped, the mud bubbled and boiled. Little bits leaped out of the tub, reminding Ford of Fourth of July sparklers.

Within minutes the mud was gone, and wisps of dust were whirling away to join the already dusty Martian atmosphere.

He showed the tub and its dusty residue to Rooney.

"Mud became dust when the West Side ceiling was breached. But P.L. Scott drowned in Central Park."

She didn't disagree.

Later on he showed the incriminating video to Nilo Hoberman.

"Okay, he drowned," said his apprentice while dutifully watching mud explode into dust. "Water in that pond is barely ankle deep. How in the world did he do it?"

"That is the sixty-four-maroon question," said Ford. "Someone moved the body, so he didn't volunteer for his trip to Heaven."

30

CENTRAL PARK was the signature structure of The Ark, a pressurized spectacle of urban engineering. Its polycarbonate roof was a shallow dome spanning more than a hundred and fifty meters without any visible support, save for slender cable stays crisscrossing the expanse on each of sixteen compass points. To Joe Ford's eyes, it looked dangerously flimsy, like everything else in this exotic village. Erected in Earth's gravity it might not have passed all the building codes, but on Mars it was a tribute to some clever architect's acute sense of elegance and economy.

Here and there hanging under the translucent surface were opaque circlets of white plastic. Ford thought they were probably intended to suggest clouds. They concealed lights and, directly overhead, the Park's famous and currently inoperable rain generating mechanism.

Ford stared up at the array of sprinkler heads above his position at the edge of the Park's extravagant half-acre pond. He was in a foul mood. Some plumbing problem had poisoned his wedding day, and he resented the failed pipes, his failed marriage, and the ridiculous superstition attached to rain in the first place.

"We've got to get up there, Nilo," he said.

"Earn ourselves some more recognition, like you said, huh?"

"Yes, and lift a curse."

Hoberman grinned. "Gee, someone else spurned by a woman."

"Don't rub it in."

Hoberman glanced upward. "Problem is, boss, those pipes are five stories up. You ready for a big lift?"

"As I'll ever be."

Hoberman turned toward the Park wall. He waved Ford to

follow and led the way to a wide door, painted to blend with the Park décor. He touched a hidden switch, and the door rolled up to reveal an industrial robot the size of a truck.

"Here's *Motro,* our portable elevator."

Hoberman opened a panel on the machine's side and extracted a small device that resembled a video game controller. He pressed a button, waited for a response, got none, and scowled.

"What now?" he groused.

Ford fired up his multiprobe and applied it to a circuit board in the machine's electronics bay.

"Main CPU is dead."

He lit his handheld flashlight and studied the dead chip.

"Wow, this guy was manufactured on Mother Earth. How old would that make it, you think? Thirty Mars years? No wonder it died."

He took a photo on his handheld and enlarged it, looking for a product code.

"We're okay," he announced at length. "Luckily for us, the dead soldier in here is a PP-020-M CPU. And we made extras."

▼

Hours later Hoberman pressed a button on the robot's portable controller, and Motro, responding to a new CPU, trundled slowly out of his garage on six hard-rubber tires.

"Repair success," declared Ford.

Out in the open the machine's color — sky blue — and its ungainly shape became visible. Motro was long and bulky. Arms ending in powerful claws were stowed along each side. A work platform riding on top made him look like a mechanical camel.

"Hey, hold up, let me try," said Ford.

Hoberman handed over the controller, and Ford used the attached joystick to maneuver Motro out to the edge of the pond.

When he was satisfied he had the robot in position directly under the malfunctioning sprinklers, he handed the controller back to his apprentice.

"That was fun," he said.

Hoberman flicked a switch on the controller, causing long stabilizer beams to rotate out of the robot's frame, anchoring it in place.

"Time to mount up, Joe."

They clambered up a ladder welded onto Motro's stern and took up positions in the work platform.

"Fasten your harness, there, Brother," commanded Hoberman. He handed Ford a hard hat and put one on himself.

Another button press started an electric motor whining somewhere inside Motro's bulk. A telescoping titanium shaft extended itself and lifted the work platform up to the ceiling.

From five stories up, the grass, the pond, the baseball diamond, and the running track blended into a beautiful design. But Ford couldn't actually look at them. The platform he was standing on was swaying back and forth, and he felt seasick.

Hoberman pointed to a ladder leading up into the sprinkler system. The bottom rung was right in front of them, chest high.

"Grab on, let's get up inside."

Ford had an urge to vomit. Yet he noticed that he didn't miss his tranquilizer pills, and the sense of freedom cheered him up.

"You've been here before."

"Yup, guilty as charged."

Ford gritted his teeth and lunged for the ladder. He climbed through the opaque plastic cloud with his eyes closed. When he opened them he could see that the water nozzles arrayed before him were all accessible via a sturdy catwalk. He stepped off the ladder onto a narrow, but solid, pathway.

Hoberman joined him a moment later. "What are we looking for?" he asked.

"Find out what's wrong. Make it rain, like it's God's fucking plan."

Hoberman shrugged. "If his plan includes the likes of us."

The problem, a fundamental one, was soon revealed. A primary valve connecting the Township's main water supply to the sprinklers was missing. The pipes were capped on either side of a twenty centimeter gap. The only water that could possibly flow ran through a secondary pipe not more than two centimeters in diameter.

"Christ almighty," growled Ford. "Now I know why it didn't rain. It can't rain. This is sabotage."

He fastened an accusing eye on Hoberman.

"You were here. Did you do this?"

Hoberman winced. "Not sure what happened," he said.

Ford decided not to pursue his suspicions while high above secure footing. He scratched his head.

"Why bother with the tiny pipe that still works? What's up with that?"

Hoberman waved an arm around. "It's a mister. Every now and then, when the humidity is just right, the spray from the secondary nozzles forms an actual cloud. From down on the ground it seems like real weather. Lots of oohs and ahhs."

Ford snorted.

"The citizens of Cratertown are easily entertained, that's for damn sure."

▼

Back down on solid ground, Ford insisted on guiding Motro into his garage. But as he turned the robot this way and that to line him up, his thumb hit the wrong button.

A semi-circular scoop rotated up and out of Motro's back. Somewhere inside his body, an electric motor began to whine, then scream. Ford clapped his hands over his ears.

zang

Motro launched a baseball out of the scoop. It skipped across the pond like a stone, arched over the baseball diamond, and bounced to a hard stop against the Park's far wall, denting the surface and chipping the paint.

"Wheeoo. . ." whistled Ford.

"Motro sometimes throws batting practice for little league kids," explained Hoberman.

"Nilo? A ball thrown that fast would kill anyone it hit. Somebody has been screwing around with Motro's settings."

Hoberman resisted the idea. "How could they?"

Ford shook his head.

"We don't know. But — now we *do know* how the West Side Auxiliary was breached. Motro did it with a baseball."

"That's crazy," said Hoberman.

Ford stared at the suspect robot.

"I was coming back from my first EVA, and I found a baseball in the dirt outside the airlock. Zoran thought kids had been fooling around out there."

"Kids will be kids," squeaked Hoberman.

Ford kicked a tire.

"Motro — this stupid industrial robot — he is the means and accessory to our murder."

The color drained from Hoberman's face. Either his mentor was losing it, or he was onto something. Scary either way.

Ford clocked his young helper's discomfort. A frosty sensation crept over him. He shivered.

"You understand, Nilo . . . Motro had help."

STEP FOUR

CRATERTOWN   191

31

THE TOWN MANAGER's avatar adopted a chipper attitude when Joe Ford and Nilo Hoberman invoked her presence in the Town Hall.

"Well, look who's here — my most frequent users in the current ninety day period."

Tammy was wearing her librarian skin, sitting at a desk with her hands folded. Behind her a wide array of shelves made it seem like her records were kept on paper, as such things had been when the Township was under construction.

Ford couldn't resist pretending that the avatar was a real person. "Good morning, Tammy. How are you today?"

"As always, Brother Ford. Personal maintenance is not required at the present moment. Thank you for asking."

"Of course."

"How may I be of service?"

Hoberman opened the Operations Manager binder to the chip catalog page.

"We want to provision the main chip printer with data for, let's see here — a PP-1000-SpF-Neural-SOC."

Tammy's face hardened.

"Neural architecture data is encrypted for security purposes. Release requires a password. Do you have it?"

Hoberman turned to page seventeen.

"I do — *KEY-H1-users* . . ."

Tammy stood up. The librarian vanished, and now Tammy was a research engineer in a white lab smock. She seemed to be surrounded by laboratory gizmos and chip manufacturing machinery.

"Place a storage device in Tray Five, please."

Hoberman dropped a tiny memory disc into Tray Five.

Tammy held up a virtual sheet of paper and fed it into the input slot of a virtual scanner.

The scanner hummed, and Hoberman's disc vibrated.

"There you are, gentlemen. Print at your pleasure from Main Chip Print Unit Oh-Thirty-One."

Ford cleared his throat.

"Thank you, Tammy. Next request. We need the data for a primary water shutoff valve. Biggest one you've got.

Tammy was suddenly clad in a greasy jumpsuit and standing in a virtual warehouse. She lifted a sheet of virtual paper from a grimy workbench and appeared to read from it.

"I show habitat pipe specifications in two, three, and five centimeters. Water mains in eighteen centimeters, and sewage cloacas in fifteen centimeters. What will you have?"

Pipe diameter — five centimeters sounds right."

Tammy ran a finger down the page.

"Now thread pitch — that's easy — all sizes turn at nine per centimeter."

"Right, thread pitch — nine turns per centimeter. What have you got for me?"

Tammy turned to the virtual storage bins behind her.

"Searching . . ." she said.

She rattled the pipes, pipe fittings, pipe couplings, pipe elbows, pipe flanges, and pipe seals in several virtual bins before turning back to face her inquisitors. She affected a regretful expression.

"I am sorry to report that I do not have any data for the valve you have described."

"Well, damn. You sure? Run a deep search."

Tammy glowered.

"I am very sure. I believe the valve in question was designed for continuous operation for one hundred Mars years. It is too simple to fail. No data required."

"Well, fuck me."

"Such talk, Brother Ford. Really, show some courtesy."

▼

Ford made a call and located Hesperia Dale wrangling a gaggle of children in the Township Zoo. They were running around in a circular room in the company of virtual lions and zebras.

Dale touched a button on her program controller. "Ooh, Kids, here comes an elephant."

Sure enough, a very large virtual beast lumbered into the lion pride, trumpeting loudly and scattering the cats. The children backed away and clustered tightly around Dale. The younger ones grabbed her knees and hid behind her legs in what might have been utter terror, except they were all giggling.

Dale nodded to Ford as he joined the party.

"Okay, children. That's it for today." She flipped a switch on her programmer and the animals vanished. "Where on Big Blue would you find lions and zebras and elephants? Anyone?"

"Africa!" they shouted in chorus.

"Right. Now shoo, off you go, and see you next week for an underwater adventure."

The children filed out of the room, all of them eyeing Ford suspiciously.

"Hello, Joe. What's up?"

Ford swung an arm around the now featureless room.

"Another one of your jobs? You're a busy woman."

Dale smiled. "I suppose. Aside from our bees, the natural world is pretty bleak here. And the kids need to understand their heritage."

"How about you? Ever think about Earth? Traveling there?"

"Now and then," she confessed. "I'd love to see a whale."

"Never too late. I might go with you, show you the sights."

"If I could even stand up in Earth gravity."

She posed to model her skinny frame.

Ford grinned. "Oh, give yourself a week, you'd get by."

She tossed her head. "A nice fantasy. Here and now, though, why the visit? All the tech that goes into the Zoo — miracle of miracles — works perfectly."

Ford removed a short length of pipe, a pipe coupling, and a small valve body from a backpack.

"I need a replacement water valve." He handed her the metal parts. "It needs to fit onto pipe like this — five centimeter main, nine thread turns per centimeter."

Dale puzzled over the steel specimen. "I'm no plumber, Joe. Explain?"

He tapped the valve body. "Here's the concept, but this one fits on two centimeter pipe. I need it scaled up for five."

Dale frowned.

"You're a designer, right?" urged Ford. "Build shapes in your computer, print out full-size chairs and so on. I thought maybe you could solve my problem."

Dale nodded. "Maybe. I sometimes print metal objects. What's it for, this valve? Why doesn't the Town Manager have the files?"

Ford colored. "Good questions. I can't really explain. Not yet anyway. Embarrassing, I know, but it's for a good cause."

Dale weighed the sample pieces doubtfully and dropped them into her carry bag.

"It better be."

She shouldered her bag and marched away into heavy afternoon foot traffic on North Axis Prom.

32

A ROBOTIC TUG was dispatched in early afternoon to tow a load of carbon fiber structures to the Habitat Outpost, a small settlement abutting the rim of Klickitat Crater, some twenty kliks north of the Township proper. About halfway along the track it stopped moving.

Ed Imowelo called upon Joe Ford to solve the problem.

"What, exactly, *is* the problem, Ed?"

"Looks like the battery died. That's my guess."

"What's the readout?"

"I don't have telemetry. Loss of power killed the signal, so I can't tell."

Ford dug into the vehicle's maintenance log on the rover shop computer.

"Says here you sent the tug out half-charged. Maybe less."

Imowelo nodded. "Trivium did the prep. Not my most reliable man."

"So . . . what's the plan?"

Imowelo's shoulders sagged. He swiped a finger across the computer screen to bring the tug's cargo manifest into view. He pointed at it.

"Outpost has a temporary skin up on the new wing they're putting in. They need permanent parts. And they finally came down from Phobos on the ferry — last transfer from the cycler that brought you here."

"And . . ."

"There's a big risk with the temp skin. We've got to move those moldings and frames and siding pieces."

"Put that dope Trivium in a rover and send him out there to

finish the tow."

Imowelo gave Ford a sheepish look. "Trivium and Nilo are out at Flight Ops, refueling the ferry. Lycus is on his way to the power station." He spread his hands. "That leaves you."

"Shit, I hate EVAs."

"Look on the bright side — you'll get to see the Outpost — that's worth a trip. Maybe check out the diamond mine and our water plant while you're at it."

▼

The dead robo tug was just coming into view when Ford's rover also died.

"Jesus fucking power fart," he exclaimed. He jammed his helmet down over his face and clamped it to his pressure suit.

"Oh man," he muttered, "how bad is it?"

He hovered a finger above the rover's exit button. If he opened the hatch, would he have enough juice to close it again? He shook his head, grumbling over his own timidity, and jabbed hard.

The hatch yawned open, and Ford stepped out onto the crater floor carrying an exposure jacket, which he laid out behind the rover's rear wheels. He was preparing to kneel down and examine the battery terminals when a wisp of smoke distracted him.

"What the hell . . ."

Some small object was fuming about a hundred yards behind the rover. Ford shrugged himself into the exposure jacket and marched back along the sandy track.

"Be damned," he said.

Lying in the soil was a cylinder about the size of a bucket handle. Bubbles were forming and popping on its plastic surface. Heavy duty terminal wires emerged from each end of the cylinder, blackened from a power overload. Ford held a hand over the device. Scorching heat made him draw his glove back to save it from melting.

"Well, shit, I am so fucked . . ." he swore.

Back inside the rover, he checked his power supply. The main propulsion battery was dead, but the auxiliary still held a charge.

With a resigned sigh he closed the hatch, opened up his radio and made a call:

> *Mayday!, Mayday!*
>
> *Joe Ford here. I'm about — let's see — about halfway to the Outpost. Ten kliks outbound. My rover's main battery has died. Say again — Mayday! — battery dead. It's too far to get there on foot or walk back, so I'm stranded with a very limited supply of oxygen. Need some help soonest, or I'll be as dead as my battery.*

33

THE WATER VALVE design requested by Hesperia Dale's estranged husband was finished before lunch, and she printed the first prototype a few hours later.

The valve body turned inside its casing, but it didn't fit tight enough to control a flow of liquid.

"Damn, it's loose," she griped. "And if at first you don't succeed . . ."

She bagged the misaligned parts and turned to leave the print shop for her home office.

". . . you try, try again . . ."

She halted at the door, considered her various obligations, and strode away in the opposite direction, toward the Farm.

". . . later, after more important tasks."

The Farm had its own small rover parked in the Secondary West Side Airlock. Dale fired it up and drove out past the main buildings to the Farm, where she cruised slowly around the perimeter on her weekly inspection, looking for air leaks, root damage, possible meteor strikes.

While she was driving, she was careful to monitor range safety radio traffic, just in case an unexpected bulletin from Ed Imowelo forecast a major sun flare and sent her scurrying back inside the Township's protective shield.

No sun flares today, however. The weather in space was calm.

She was finishing her first pass along the Farm's border when her radio squealed.

Uh-oh, was she in trouble?

Hesperia to Rover Tower. Ed? Hello? What's up?

Imowelo did not reply.

"Not you, Ed. Then who?" She fiddled around with her radio controls and called up the transmitter ID.

"Huh, another rover. One-Zero-Two, sounds like, sending me a really crappy signal. Where are you, buddy?"

She toggled her microphone.

> *Rover One-Oh-Two, talk to me.*

> *Brazz . . . May-dazz . . . Fazz here . . . Outpost track . . . . stalled for loss of power-zazz . . .*

Dale's brow creased as she focused on the scratchy signal.

> *Joe Ford? That you? Go ahead.*

> *Hesper? Hey — I'm stuck halfway to the Zazz-post. No response from anyone. Rovers all in service. Mayday. Low oxy-jazz . . . krazz . . . razz . . .*

Dale felt her arms grow cold.

> *Hesperia to Rover Tower. Ed, you there? Need a backup rover to the Outpost. Brother Ford is sending Mayday and he needs help ASAP. Ed, hear me? Talk back.*

She waited for a full minute, but Ed Imowelo did not respond.

She glanced down at her instruments, assessing her power supply. Hmm, twenty kliks to the Outpost. Enough juice, but not much to spare.

> *Joe? Hang in there, breath easy, I'm on my way.*

Getting to Ford's location as quickly as possible with enough electricity left over to reach the Outpost required careful attention to power management. She punched in some numbers on the rover's keypad and learned that nineteen kliks per hour was the best tradeoff between speed and wattage.

She set the throttle and headed north.

> *Rover Tower? Hesperia to Imowelo. New drive plan, destination Outpost. Come back?*

No one replied for several minutes. Finally, just as Dale hit the main trail winding north, her radio receiver crackled.

> *Imowelo to Dale. Watch your meters, Sister. I'm doing sim calculations, and your little donkey will be running on neutrinos before you arrive if you're not awfully careful.*

Imowelo was himself being careful to dot his protocol I-s and cross his responsibility T-s.

> *Hey, Ed, thanks for the tip, I'm good.*

> *Be advised — we don't have spare rescue wheels available at this time.*

Dale tightened her grip on the steering yoke.

> *Won't need them . . .*

she declared in a bold voice. She didn't actually feel very bold.

After half an hour of anxious travel, she got her first glimpse of the broken down robo tug and Joe Ford's equally immobilized rover, both taking shape behind the gradually parting curtain of dusty Martian air.

Ten minutes later she pulled up alongside. She buttoned up her pressure suit, set her rad tag, and hiked a few yards to Ford's machine. There she put her helmet against the rover's driver side window and peered into the cockpit. Two layers of reflective polymer obscured all interior detail, and where the hell was Brother Ford? But within a few seconds she detected the outlines of a suited figure slumped against the far window.

"Hey, Joe!"

The figure did not stir.

"Wake up, Joe!"

She pounded on the window. Pounded again and again.

"Joe Ford! Joe! Wake the fuck up, Joe!"

No result. Worse, the figure was not wearing a helmet. Where was it? Dale moved her head around to see at different angles, but couldn't locate it.

If she opened the rover hatch from outside, Ford would be subject to Mars' tenuous and oxygen-free atmosphere, a near vacuum. Be exposed very long and his blood would boil.

She thought about the problem for a few seconds, then — *"Goddammit!"* — she jerked the hatch open and tumbled inside.

She slammed the hatch shut with one hand, undid her helmet with the other, turned her air supply to max flow, clamped her own helmet onto Joe Ford's neck ring, held her breath, and prayed.

She thought her head would explode, but instead the oxygen from her suit filled the compact rover cabin, allowing her to breathe a heartfelt sigh of relief. She removed her helmet from Ford's suit.

"Hey, Bro, wake up already!" She grabbed a thatch of Ford's curly hair and pulled his head upright. His eyes popped open.

"Ouch," said Ford.

Dale nearly fainted. "You, you asshole, you nearly got yourself killed."

Ford nodded. "Yup." — he showed her the cylindrical item he had found out on the track — "I didn't account for sabotage."

Dale took the cylinder out of Ford's hand and gave it a good once over. "What is it?"

"A big electrical resistor, industrial grade."

"Yeah?"

"Soldered in between my power pack and my motor, it drained all the energy by slowly getting red hot."

Dale smacked the thing against her knee. "Somebody did this? Deliberately?"

"'Fraid so. Doesn't speak well of the Friends, does it?"

Dale scowled. "Five more minutes, five more max, they would have had you."

She reached between the seats and opened a panel in the floorboards.

"Something you should know . . ."

She lifted an oxygen bottle into view.

"See? Emergency air supply."

Ford bowed his head. "I am an idiot."

Dale grinned. "Let's not debate the point. The big question right now is, go back or go on?"

Ford looked around. Up ahead he could see habitat parts packed aboard the trailer that was sitting behind the stalled-out robo tug.

"I was hoping to get a look at your wicked Outpost, see how it compares to Las Vegas."

"I've heard of that city. We're taught that it's the work of the devil himself, like all of Earth, only worse. You been there?"

"Of course. Several times."

"Well then, on we go."

▼

Dale and Ford arrived at the Outpost just after sunset with habitat parts in tow and a five percent charge on their power pack.

On the way they passed what looked like a petroleum tank farm to Ford. Large steel globes and tall silos surrounding a pressurized building complex; a labyrinth of pumps and pipes; an aqueduct running south.

"Water plant?" he asked.

"Good guess."

"Why all the tanks?"

"We separate the heavy water — which, you may have heard, is a lot more abundant on Mars than on Earth. Then we extract the deuterium gas, compress it into carbon fiber tanks, and ship it to Earth for their fusion reactors."

"Mmm . . ."

"It's our big export."

Ford nodded. "What about the diamond mine? Every woman on Earth wants a Martian stone on her ring."

Dale pointed toward Klickitat Crater's rim, away to the northwest of their position.

"Earthmoving robots are working to excavate our famous gems inside the throat of that small volcano you can just make out on top of the wall there."

"I know those things are pretty rare . . . and also seriously buckworthy. I couldn't afford one for you."

Dale chuckled.

"What a tightwad you turned out to be."

▼

The Outpost, Ford discovered, was everything gossip and rumors had led him to expect. Small and cozy rather than large and impersonal. Free of moral rules and regulations.

The central atrium food stalls served the usual plant-based fare (presumably grown on Dale's Farm), but also a decent pint of beer.

A pickup band was playing dance music, and Ford was amazed to see several couples stepping to the beat on the outpost's small and well-worn dance floor.

Dale touched Ford's sleeve and joined them, twirling into their midst, arms waving, hips swaying.

Ford was mesmerized by her performance. Given his bitter experience with their arranged marriage, he had booked her as a cold prude. He was starting to think that he might have to revise his assessment.

Dale armwaved an invitation to join her. He swallowed hard and pretended he didn't see her gesture. As the tune progressed she worked her way to where he was awkwardly standing and dragged him into the group.

"I don't dance," he protested. "Never have."

"Past tense. This is now. Count four, move your feet. Here, put your arms around me."

She positioned one of Ford's hands at the small of her back and clasped his other hand in hers.

"There. How hard was that?"

"This is embarrassing."

Dale tilted her head toward the onlookers.

"See any critics? We're invisible."

Indeed, most of the people who weren't actually dancing were too busy with their food and drink to pay any attention to Ford and his clumsy feet.

When the song ended, Ford broke away, grateful for the chance to escape, but Dale grabbed a hand and yanked him back onto the floor.

Halfway through the second number he began to relax.

"You shuffle very well," said Dale.

"Ha-ha," replied Ford. But truthfully, he was beginning to

enjoy himself. The tall woman in his arms felt lighter than air.

They moved through a slow number without speaking, each lost in thought.

"Time for food," decided Dale, breaking the spell.

They ordered plant burgers and beers and consumed them at a tiny table in a corner of the hall, enmity and mistrust thrust aside by the alchemical magic of their unfamiliar circumstances.

"Where — how — do we spend the night?" wondered Ford. "I don't see any motel signs."

Dale looked him over. "Don't get your hopes up, big guy."

Ford blanched. "What hopes, Hes? In case you're wondering, I don't have any. I'm just really tired."

After learning that no rooms were available, they wound up sharing Dale's rover. The proprietor of the Outpost MicroMart lent them a heavy quilt that encouraged sharing.

They woke up in the morning hugging each other against bone-chilling outside temperatures. Once their heads cleared they scrambled to untangle themselves.

"Sorry, sorry. Didn't mean to crowd you."

"My fault, it's cold outside."

They each apologized several times. Then they charged up the rover and drove back to The Ark.

The trip was routine. No incidents and not much conversation.

34

T HUVIA , that you ?"

Dr. Rooney was doing paperwork when her office door opened and Thuvia Lofgren sneaked inside.

Lofgren put a finger to her lips. "Shhh . . . don't give me away."

"I wouldn't dream of it. Let's have a look at you, check on that baby you've got riding inside."

She readied her stethoscope, but before she got very far into her exam, Joe Ford showed up.

"Why, hello, Sister Lofgren."

"Agh . . . please don't tell Zoran you saw me here."

Ford leaned over Rooney and gave her an affectionate kiss.

"Morning, babe. Thanks for letting me sleep."

Lofgren bounced in her seat. "Ooh, you two! Wow! Did not know about this! Did not guess!"

Rooney shifted her weight and frowned at her lover.

Ford caught the hint. "I won't tell on you, Thuvia, if you don't tell on us. Fair deal?"

Thuvia waggled her head. She groaned in journalistic despair. "This is hard — you're a great story, best I've heard in months."

"And you are going to ignore it."

"Mmm . . . geez . . . well . . . *okay.*"

Ford pointed to the infirmary and its hospital beds. He waved his multiprobe toward Rooney.

"Sorry to get in your way. I'm just here to fix a thristle pin."

"Whatever that is," said Rooney.

"Nothing, really. Mythical. Shouldn't take long."

Ford entered the infirmary, shut the door behind him, and sat himself down on the nearest bed. He plugged the leads from his multiprobe into a wall socket, waited for the device to power up, then initiated a call to Earth.

> *Blue Eyes to BlueTalk . . . confirm Protocol Two.*
> *Death of P.L. Scott is foul play for sure, and I have the evidence:*
> *One – Scott was a dissident threat to Like-Minded rule.*
> *Two – The place of his demise was faked with a meteorite that fell more than nine years ago.*
> *Three – autopsy shows dust in his lungs, but it started out as mud. Body was moved by perp or perps.*
> *Now — I myself have been subject to attempted murder by sabotage of a long range rover I was driving.*
> *Keep those marines ready for action.*
> *Blue Eyes out.*

▼

"Who is it? Do you have an appointment?" queried the door to the Founder's apartment in blunt tones designed to deflect unwanted solicitations.

"No, I don't," admitted Ford. "But I have urgent business that concerns your Founder."

"Please wait," said the door.

A minute later the door zipped aside, revealing Lycus Salazar showing a skeptical frown.

"Brother Ford. What is so urgent that brings you to us unannounced?"

Ford showed Salazar the electrical resistor that nearly cost him his life. "Security," he said.

The Active Deacon eyed the device doubtfully. "What is it?"

"Electrical resistor. Normally used on the main transmission lines from Township reactors" — he paused — "and it fell off my rover."

Salazar hesitated, his brow wrinkled in thought.

"Wait here."

The door closed in Ford's face. He was left to cool his heels for five long minutes. Just as his patience was wearing out, the door reopened. Salazar beckoned him inside.

"The Founder will see you. Come with me."

Ford followed Salazar into the Founder's sumptuous atrium. He was there before, and so not shocked by the luxury, but he now noticed something else: birdsong. Speakers hidden under the foliage were piping out calls and elaborate songs. Among them he recognized the complex trills of a house finch.

"Hello, Brother Ford," came a booming voice.

Ford turned to see the Founder wheeling his way. He made a deferential salute. Salazar remained in the background long enough to be satisfied that no harm would come to the old man, then disappeared into one of the apartment's several rooms.

"Let me look at you," said the Founder. "Still alive, I see, and glad I am of that."

He pointed to his poolside bench. Ford followed, but remained standing.

"Something you should see" — Ford handed him the resistor — "this is a murder weapon."

The Founder laughed. "A prank, more likely. Someone having a joke at your expense."

"Sir . . ?"

"My Active Deacons are young, inexperienced, impulsive."

Ford retrieved the resistor. "I understand why your acolytes might resent my presence here. Know this — unless you reassure me of my personal safety, I won't make my proof-of-life calls, and you'll be dealing with the military arm of the Planetary Settlement Agency."

Ford thought he had landed a decisive blow, but the Founder seemed unimpressed. He looked at Ford. His expression was pitiful. "I have dealt with the PSA from time to time. I believe I could persuade them to call off their dogs, should it come to that."

Ford was stunned by the Founder's nonchalance.

"As you please, sir. I see you're a gambling man."

"Indeed," said the Founder. He rolled his chair halfway around the pool.

"Look here. You're a maintenance engineer. My fountain has stopped working. All this plumbing, what's wrong?"

Ford examined the fountain controls. He noticed an electrical panel set into the pool rim. He opened it and located a circuit breaker inside, tripped by an overload.

"Your fountain motor is working too hard," he said.

He opened a panel on the floor. There inside he discovered a valve.

"Here we go — I'm going to reduce the water flow here, take a load off your motor. Should do the trick."

He twisted the valve handle, observing that the device controlling the water supply to the Founder's pool looked suspiciously like it might have been cut from the rain cloud in Central Park.

"Your controls look well set up, well maintained. Who is it does such good work?"

The Founder beamed. "Why, young Hoberman. Your apprentice, I believe?"

"That's right. Energetic guy, quick study, capable. Asset to the Township," praised Ford.

"Glad to hear it. One of our own taking responsibility, makes me proud."

"As well it should."

He reset the circuit breaker. The fountain immediately bubbled up, spraying water droplets around the pool in a beautiful pattern of interlocking rosettes.

The Founder breathed a sigh of satisfaction.

"Thank you, Brother Ford. Thank you very much."

"Not at all. Happy to help."

Ford dipped his head in a show of respect and was quick to take his leave.

35

PHOBOS was gliding overhead, but when the routine line-of-sight transmission from the Town Manager didn't connect to Phobos Station, Joe Ford and Nilo Hoberman were dispatched to South End Avenue to perform a fix.

The antenna stem rose up like a tree trunk through the ceiling just inside the outer wall. Ford opened an access panel, and handed his system analyzer to Hoberman.

"Tell me what's wrong."

His apprentice applied the analyzer leads to cables emerging from the antenna's power supply. When the readout registered normal output, he poked at exposed electrical leads on the main circuit board's radio transmitter chips.

"Uh-oh. Bad modulator," he announced, popping a daughterboard free. "We need one of our standard PP-020-M CPU replacements."

Ford reached into his carry bag. "And I happened to bring one of our spares." He passed it to Hoberman, who snapped it into place.

Ford called the Town Manager on his handheld.

"Tammy, old girl. Try Phobos now. Let me know how it goes."

Mere seconds later the Town Manager returned Ford's call with thumbs-up news.

Hoberman closed the antenna access panel.

Ford retrieved his analyzer and clipped it to his belt.

"Good diagnosis. Looks like you know your way around."

"Thank you, Joe."

"I'm impressed."

Hoberman detected a sour note in Ford's voice. "Nice to hear," he mumbled.

Ford touched a thoughtful finger to his nose. "Yes, very impressed. But . . . not all in a good way."

"Beg pardon?"

"I was adjusting water flow in the Founder's pool. The valve appears to have been liberated from the rain machine in the Park."

"Really."

"You were up there. You cut it out to operate the Founder's private fountain."

Hoberman flushed red. "Not true! Talk to Ed Imowelo, he engineered that fountain." The apprentice sounded fierce, but he couldn't meet Ford's accusing gaze.

"Don't lie to me, Kid. Imowelo might have designed it all, but you did the dirty work."

Hoberman teetered on his heels, shuffled to a nearby bench, and collapsed on it, lolling like a puppet with its strings cut.

"There was no print pattern for the valve," muttered the apprentice. "Hard to say no to the Founder."

"Ahh, that's better — a confession," declared Ford.

Hoberman dropped his head into his hands and stared at the floor.

"And," Ford continued, "Now that I'm getting to know the real you, I'm betting you planted that meteor in the West Side Auxiliary to make it look like P.L. Scott died in a vacuum there."

"Um . . ."

"Come on, Boy, out with it," Ford commanded.

"Yeah . . . all right, okay . . . . . . I did it."

"That act, in case you're wondering, is a crime, a felony — accessory to murder after the fact."

Hoberman moaned.

"Who told you to do it?" demanded Ford.

"Lycus."

"Who told him?"

Hoberman wiped salty tears from his eyes. "I don't know. Ismenius, maybe?"

"Maybe. We'll find out. You knew all this the moment you went to work with me, and concealed it."

"Ismenius told me to be careful."

"Careful?" snorted Ford.

"I think he said, *circumspect,* one of his big words."

Ford paced back and forth, gathering his thoughts. "Jesus fucking Judas," he growled.

He stopped in front of his guilt-ridden companion, reached out a hand and yanked him upright.

"Because you came clean, I'm going to give you the benefit of my very big doubts."

Hoberman stole a fearful sidelong look at his mentor.

"I'll let you off the hook," — Ford pressed a finger against Hoberman's chest — "but from here on out, you're going to live up to Like-Minded ideals, and more important, you're going to work for me."

Hoberman gagged. "The Friends . . ."

"What?"

"They'll beat me up."

Ford took Hoberman by the shoulders and shook him. "No, they won't. We've got a murder on our hands. We're going to override the terror squad. Bring regime change to fucking Cratertown."

36

DR. ROONEY locked her office desk, shed her medical smock, and turned off the lights. She exited onto Interplanetary Highway where it met East Side Boulevard and, following medical protocol, locked her office door.

She checked her watch — whoa, late — and placed a call to Joe Ford's handheld. The call went straight to voicemail.

"Joe? It's me. Dinner date? I got stuck on paperwork, but I'm on my way. Meet you in the Food Hall."

The Hall was crowded with hungry diners and loud with cheerful after-work chatter. Joe Ford was not there to greet her.

She called him again. "Hey, babe, I'm here. Where are you?"

No answer.

"Damn."

She shook her handheld and made another call.

"Nilo? I'm looking for Joe, and he's not picking up. Where are you guys?"

Nilo Hoberman was a hundred meters away on South Axis Promenade.

"I'm walking toward the Food Hall, but your old man is not with me."

"Where did he go?"

"Not sure. We were lubing a rover gearbox. Haven't seen him since. An hour or so."

"Christ. Keep an eye out, okay? We're supposed to be on the town — heavy date — and I'm being stood up."

Hoberman chuckled. "Will do. Better cool those jets, Doc."

He continued on northward while making a call of his own.

"Hey, Joe, your main squeeze is wondering about you. No one

is paying for overtime labor. What's up? Need some help?"

Ford did not answer.

Hoberman pocketed his handheld and came to a sudden stop. Just ahead a crowd of homeward bound citizens had divided themselves into two groups. They were milling about, yelling at each other and pointing fingers.

Hoberman thought he could distinguish angry dissidents on one side from equally irate loyalists on the other.

"It's murder," shouted one of the evident dissidents.

"Ridiculous rumor. You're an ass to believe it!" returned a member of the loyalist faction.

"Ass am I? Who's the moron covering for the Friends and their stupid anarchy? Huh?"

"Watch your mouth, pal!"

"Anarchy! Anarchy!" chanted the dissidents.

"Heresy! Traitors! Scum! Maybe the Outpost will have you! We won't!"

Now the pushing and shoving began. Punches were thrown, hair was pulled. Hoberman raised his arms and marched in between the factions.

"Stop!" he shouted. "I am an Active Deacon, and I'm here to insist — no brawling in The Ark!"

Men and women from both factions seized Hoberman by his clothing and threw him out of their midst. He smacked against the corridor wall and crashed to the floor. Someone kicked him hard before the assailant's comrades managed to intervene.

Hoberman crawled a few meters, got to his feet, and quickstepped out of reach.

Behind him, the scuffle resumed. Yelling, punching, kicking, wrestling on the floor.

Hoberman was shocked by the sudden rip in The Ark's social

fabric. He dialed a call on his handheld with shaking fingers.

"My God, Liko — there's a *riot* down on South Prom. Unheard of! You won't believe it. Get Ismenius, get Triv, get down here."

▼

Rooney was cooling her heels at a table for two in the Food Hall, nursing a glass of fruit punch. Her failure to raise Joe Ford by telephone caused ugly suspicions to take form and kindle an unwanted pang of jealousy.

"You don't suppose?" she said aloud, cursing her unworthy feelings.

She rose from her chair and made her way down Interplanetary Highway to the East Residence district. There she pounded on Hesperia Dale's front door.

"Hesper, open up — it's Dana."

After a suspenseful beat, the door opened wide.

"Hi, Doc," said Dale. She stared at Rooney's troubled face. "What's wrong?"

"Is Joe in there with you? Is that what's going on?"

Dale was taken aback by the implied accusation. She felt her face redden.

"Don't be silly. My estranged husband is wherever he is. I have no idea."

Rooney tilted her head to see past Dale and into her unit.

Dale stood aside to allow it. "Jesus, Dana. He's not here. I am working on one of his projects, though — a replacement valve — and that's the sum total of our relationship."

Rooney seemed to relax. "Yeah, I'm being paranoid."

"You sure are. If I gave a damn, I'd be the jealous one, not you."

"Sorry, Hes. He's late for a dinner we planned, he won't answer my calls, and Nilo can't find him either."

She pivoted on a heel and trudged back the way she came.

Dale was closing her door when the import of Rooney's visit hit her.

"Hey, Dana — call me when he turns up, okay?"

Rooney made a tired finger wave of acknowledgment without turning around.

▼

As she arrived back at the Food Hall she was flagged down by Hoberman, Salazar, and Counselor Pomerance. They were each shepherding citizens hurt in the riot.

"Dr. Rooney!" called Pomerance. "Are we glad to see you. Can you open the infirmary? We've got injuries here. Bruises, broken nose, scraped knuckles. Nothing fatal, but — "

" — Let me have a look."

Rooney performed a quick assessment. She shook her head in wonderment.

"Good Christ. At least I don't see bite marks. Follow me . . ."

She led the parade of suffering to her office and there bound up the unruly citizens' superficial wounds.

"You guys are a disgrace. *Fighting!* If it weren't a scandal, I'd be laughing out loud at your ridiculous behavior. Hippocratic Oath be damned, I'm inclined to let you stew in your own blood."

But of course she administered lidocaine, handed out pain pills, extra bandages, and made sure the combatants were all safe and comfortable.

For a while she was too busy to worry about Joe Ford and his whereabouts.

37

COUNSELOR POMERANCE was in his office doing paperwork. He couldn't concentrate on his order forms and export manifests, however, because he couldn't wrestle his mind away from speculating about last night's riot. A silly incident on the one hand, but the harbinger of a dimly foreseen crisis on the other. What crisis? What was the issue dividing his citizens? Why the anger? The rage? The likely result?

He was unable to harness his thoughts or tease out their meaning, because someone was knocking on his door.

"Come in," he said. "It's always open."

Lycus Salazar stuck his head around the door's edge. "Not too busy, Counselor? Got a minute?"

Pomerance rubbed his eyes and waved the Active Deacon inside. "Please." He gestured toward Dale's prototype chair. "Take a seat."

Salazar remained standing.

"You okay, Brother? You look troubled."

Pomerance shrugged. "Don't worry about me. What's on your mind?

I . . . um . . . I found something. And, um, I thought you might like to have it."

Pomerance sat up straight. "Something? What? Hand it over."

"Right" — Salazar removed an object from his carry bag — "It's the Earthman's tool. He uses it for everything — system analyzer, circuit tracer, but also a radio, and given the right configuration, a taser."

"Taser? You sure? How do you know that?"

"He tased me out on the Farm."

222

Pomerance nodded. "The Mayfield discipline. God save us."

"Yes, sir."

Pomerance took the object from Salazar. He turned it over in his hands, inspecting the dials and buttons, peering closely at the tiny display screen.

"Ford's magic wand," he said. He pulled a pair of power leads out of the handle and regarded them doubtfully. "Have you tried operating this thing?"

"No, sir."

"Where did you find it?"

Salazar hesitated. Pomerance saw a guilty look pass across the Active Deacon's face.

"No — don't tell me. I don't want to know."

Salazar hastened to explain himself. "I guess Brother Ford misplaced it, and we just happened along at the right time."

Pomerance pressed a button on the probe. A tiny LED blinked, but nothing else happened.

"Good work, Liko. Tricky for us to use, but this should crimp our new friend's style."

Salazar shuffled his feet.

"Maybe Brother Ford had an accident and dropped his tool. Maybe . . . maybe it was a serious accident."

"I hope not." He studied Salazar for signs of evasion. "It's not wise to speculate, Liko. As Counselor I must take a hopeful view."

"Understood. Forgive me if I don't agree."

Pomerance placed Ford's probe on his desk. He knitted his hands behind his head.

"Tell me, you were there — what is your view of last night's disturbance?"

Salazar shook his head. "I can't figure it out. The Earthman's evil influence?"

Pomerance pursed his lips. "Not very charitable to say that. We must temper realism with optimism."

"We hear that Dr. Rooney is returning to Earth on the next cycler," mused Salazar. "We also hear that she and Brother Ford are, um, very good friends."

"I hear the same thing," allowed Pomerance with a wink. "The sordid reality of human relations."

"Maybe Brother Ford will go with her," suggested Salazar, adding "If he's well enough to travel."

"See? That's optimism."

38

JOE FORD woke up slowly and in pain. His head was throbbing. He touched his face, where a large lump bulged from his brow. His throat was burning. His eyes seemed to be glued shut. He struggled to pry them open and check his surroundings.

He was lying on the floor of a windowless freight rover.

"Must have fallen," he mumbled.

He groaned and sat up.

"Where am I?"

The interior was almost featureless. The only cargo was a stack of empty hydrogen tanks and a pile of dried-out water bladders. Some of the floorboards were torn up. Wires protruded from an open panel on one wall.

"Rover shop, or maybe the ferry hangar. Freighter Six-Zero, in for maintenance. Hah, Sexy Sixty, always breaking down."

He felt around for his multiprobe and his handheld telephone. Both, he soon discovered, were nowhere to be found.

"Damn."

He turned around to face the freighter's forward bulkhead and the entry hatch. He paused to listen for activity in the bay outside, but heard nothing.

He twisted the hatch lock handle, withdrawing six steel pins from the freighter's frame. He cracked it open. Surprise — air whistled through the gap, rushing out of the rover and into the near vacuum of the hangar itself. Ford yanked the hatch shut just in time.

"Good God."

He figured half his oxygen was gone in less than ten seconds. He stood up and bounced against the wall. His head was spinning.

226

He put a hand out. The freighter walls were well insulated, but his hand came away cold. Evidently the rover shop's outer door was wide open to the rigors of the Martian environment.

He groped his way to the rear of the freighter, where a pair of green oxygen tanks were sticking up from an opening in the floor. One of the tanks was empty with its valve left open. He surmised that he owed his life to the vented gas. What kind soul had decided to spare him, he wondered.

He opened the valve on the second tank. Oxygen flowed noisily for several minutes, then slowed, sighed, and stopped.

He had no way to measure the pressure, but it was pretty clear he was breathing on borrowed time.

"How did I get here?" he grumbled.

▼

Twenty-four hours and forty minutes earlier, Joe Ford was called to the ferry hangar to repair a freight trailer. When he opened the freighter's hatch, an invisible cloud of hydrogen gas erupted. He stumbled and fell inside the vehicle, out cold from the oxygen deprived interior.

And here came two men, Lycus Salazar and Trivium Quinn, in pressure suits buttoned up tight. They pushed Ford's inert body all the way inside the freighter.

"I dunno," worried Quinn, "the hydrogen didn't catch fire. He didn't burn up like you planned."

"Doesn't matter," replied Salazar. "He's out." He located an oxygen cylinder in the rear of the freighter and opened the valve.

"What? What are you doing?" griped Quinn

"We're not murderers, Triv. We can fix it so he does the job himself."

Salazar picked up Ford's multiprobe and his handheld

telephone off the freighter floor.

"Look what I found," he chortled.

Back outside, he pressed a button on the freighter's hull to close the hatch, then pressed another button on a hangar support column. Motors whirred, and the hangar door slowly cranked itself open. All the air inside rushed out.

"Think about it, Triv. Pretty soon Ford wakes up — if he didn't get burned too bad when the hydrogen hit his mucus membranes and turned to acid. Now he opens the trailer hatch . . ."

Salazar didn't bother to complete the thought.

"Why would he open the hatch without a suit on?" protested Quinn, tapping the side of his helmet.

"Because, you dope, he won't know the hangar isn't pressurized."

39

TRAPPED inside the freighter, Joe Ford was well aware of his desperate situation. A vacuum in the ferry hangar, precious little oxygen in his temporary prison, and no windows.

"I can't fix what I can't see," he groaned.

He shuffled toward the rear of the freighter, where loose wires were sticking out of an open panel in the wall. He fingered them, touching each in turn.

"Ow," he said. Two of the wires delivered low voltage shocks.

"What else have we got?" he wondered.

He pushed a pile of empty water bladders aside and discovered a loose floorboard. Underneath it he could see the freighter's main power pack in its fiberglass enclosure. Tucked alongside and trailing a bundle of loose wires was a rectangular plastic box. He hauled it out. A display screen was visible on the front face, cracked and dark. A tiny plastic joystick and three buttons were located beside the screen. Obviously, it was the controller for a device of some kind. He didn't know exactly what that might be.

Ford didn't have to think very hard to mentally connect the loose wires sprouting from the open wall panel to the similarly loose wires hanging from the box and its little screen. Making the actual connections took time, however. More time than he wanted to spend. He consciously measured out each breath while he worked, anxious that each intake of the freighter's thin air might be his last.

Finally, the pair of hot wires from the wall panel were twisted correctly onto the corresponding wires from the controller, just as Ford's aching fingers refused to continue. The display lit up in full color.

"Aha!" he exclaimed.

He squatted down on the freighter floor, and pressed button number one, treating himself to a narrow view of a hangar wall. He could just barely read a notice posted there:

Suits Required at All Times.

"Yeah, suits, why don't I have one on?" he grumbled. "I am a moron, an idiot, a total asshole. And where is this fucking camera located? Wait, I know, — it's on the power umbilical. Gotta be."

He thumbed the joystick, and the view panned away from the wall, moving erratically past a nearby rover, up to the ceiling, then down to the open hangar egress door.

"Oh crap."

The joystick was wired up backwards. Pushing left tilted the camera up, pushing right tilted it down, up panned left, and down panned right.

Ford struggled to aim the camera at the umbilical socket that he knew must exist somewhere.

Outside the freighter, attached to the hull, a long flexible arm — the power umbilical — swiveled this way and that as Ford twiddled the controller's joystick. Eventually he got a glimpse of a power socket, the bullseye of a bright yellow target painted on the hangar wall above a sign reading *480 VOLTS.*

Problem: how to shove the umbilical into the socket? Moving the joystick only re-aimed the camera. But button number two caused the umbilical to pull back, and button number three extended it outward. Unfortunately, at maximum extension the socket remained out of reach.

"Shit," said Ford.

He dropped the controller and cradled his head in his hands. He was near to tears.

But he wasn't quite ready to give up. "Come on, Joe," he told himself, "for the love of God and a long life . . ."

The controller had bounced out of reach. He retrieved it by reeling in the attached wires.

"Okay, still breathing, not done yet . . ."

Now he swung the umbilical around, up, and down, looking for another socket, one within reach. He found none.

His search swept the camera past a freestanding column with some sort of metal box attached. What was that? A fire alarm? He panned back for a better look. No, not a fire alarm, just an electrical junction box for tools and work lights.

"Well, at least it's something."

He aimed the camera squarely at the box, pressed button number three and slammed the umbilical against it. The blow dented the box and killed his little screen's video signal.

He pressed button number two to retract the umbilical, then blindly slammed it forward again.

He repeated the procedure half a dozen times. On the seventh try the controller exploded from an electrical overload. Sparks flew everywhere, singeing his eyelashes. He felt the buzzing of a nearby klaxon horn vibrating through the freighter floorboards.

"Help," he said.

▼

Ten minutes later Ed Imowelo and Nilo Hoberman arrived in the hangar wearing their mandated pressure suits, bought there by the alarm Ford had blindly triggered. Imowelo levered a handle to close the hangar door. Hoberman fisted an emergency switch to restart a flow of air.

Another five minutes went by while the hangar repressurized. Once the pair was certain that it was safe, they opened the freighter hatch.

Ford was out cold on the floor inside.

Imowelo took Ford by his shoulders, and Hoberman grabbed his feet. They huffed and puffed him out of the freighter and onto a cargo cart.

Running the cart at top speed got them to the Township infirmary in ten minutes.

There Dr. Rooney applied an oxygen mask and maxed out the flow rate. Ford's chest heaved.

Almost immediately she was joined by Hesperia Dale, who was breathing hard herself, having run all the way from the Farm.

"How's he doing?"

Rooney shook her head. "Can't tell. Hypoxia, possible brain damage, could be bad."

Dale bit her lip. She placed a hand on Ford's chest, felt it rise and fall.

Rooney folded her arms to brace herself. "He's an Earther, a tough guy."

"So we watch and wait?" queried Hoberman.

"That's right," said Rooney, wiping moisture from a damp eye.

Dale wrapped her arms around the doctor. "Hey, he's an Earther, a tough guy. He's going to be okay."

The vigil continued for hours, with no hint of improvement. The two women retired to an infirmary bed and sat there, hoping for the best, pretending to be confident. Hoberman remained at Ford's bedside. Imowelo wandered away and reappeared with coffee and sandwiches.

"Whoa, hey, look here . . ." burbled Hoberman through a mouthful of avocado burger.

Ford's eyelids were fluttering. He reached up and tore the oxygen mask off.

"How long was I out?"

His companions let out a cheer.

"Too long. Hours."

Ford tried to sit up. "I smell Mars food. It's terrible, but I'm starving."

Dale pushed him back down on the bed.

"Take it easy, Tarzan."

She placed a hand under Ford's neck and raised his head. Rooney allowed him to sip a few drops of her coffee. Then she showed him a medical swab and waved it back and forth.

"Track this stick without turning your head."

Ford's eyes swiveled to follow Rooney's movements.

"Good, that's good. Now, tell me how many fingers you see."

Ford managed a wry grin.

"All six," he said.

Rooney punched his arm.

"Bad guess. Add thirteen and seven. What's the total?"

"Thirty?"

"Stop it, Joe. There's a kiss waiting if you get the next question."

"Shoot."

"Name Phobos' orbital period."

"Seven hours, thirty minutes."

Rooney lifted his left hand and kissed it.

"Close enough. I guess you'll live."

40

THE STOLEN MULTIPROBE resisted all of Counselor Pomerance's attempts to make it work.

He examined it closely, pressed buttons in various combinations, squeezed the handles, turned intriguing knobs, moved a promising slider, even connected the tool's leads to a plug under his office desk. His efforts did not achieve positive results.

"That thing . . . *diabolical,*" he concluded.

He rolled his office chair back from his desk and stared at it through suspicious eyes.

He was considering and rejecting alternative solutions to the puzzle when a knock at his door announced the probe's owner.

"Brother Ford," said Pomerance, sitting up straight in his chair. If he was surprised to see the Earthman, he was quick to suppress any visible reaction.

"We feared the worst. But here you are. Let me tell you, I am very much relieved."

"Me too," growled Ford. He pointed at the tool. "You'll never get it to work, you know."

"Well, I was hoping. It's such a versatile gadget."

"Yes it is, and I'd like it back, please."

Pomerance spread his hands out wide. "Why should I relinquish custody, may I ask? Some of my associates regard you as a very dangerous man, and this device as a weapon."

Ford adjusted the visitor chair's position and sat down. He tapped Pomerance's desk.

"Your associates are right, I am dangerous. You just don't know why."

Pomerance grimaced. "Please enlighten me . . ."

Ford indicated his tool. "My device started out as a standard voltmeter, already the latest tech on Earth of course, but also modified for me by the Planetary Settlement Agency, in case I needed some muscle. Pick it up."

Pomerance did so.

"Squeeze the handles."

"Um, okay, squeezing."

"Press buttons one and five while turning the little voltage knob to twelve."

Pomerance pressed and turned. The tiny display screen on the probe's face lit up.

"It says, *Ready to Test,*" marveled the Counselor, amazed by his easy success.

"Now clamp the leads on a power cord."

Pomerance reeled out the leads, reached under his desk, and fastened the clips to his lamp cord.

"Press button number two and move the slider to position seven."

Pomerance followed Ford's instructions, and jerked backward as a distant voice from the probe's hidden speaker jarred his customary self assurance.

> *BlueTalk to Blue Eyes — Alert — Alert — Alert*
> *Proof-of-life transmission not received. Accordingly, we are marshalling an expeditionary company of Marines. They are prepared to board a Hot Shot Transfer Vehicle that will swing them to Mars in thirty-nine days, tasked to restore order in the settlement by force.*
> *Do you retain freedom of action? If affirm, acknowledge this query soonest. Five days to launch.*

Pomerance scowled.

"Good Christ. Soldiers — *with guns*. Five days. Who's *we?*"

Ford shrugged. "The Settlement Executive Committee, I suppose. I don't know their names."

"You did this. For shame — bringing Earth's tyrants down on our heads."

Ford shook his head. "Don't give me that, Counselor. Your righteous Friends, Active Deacons, whatever you call them — they tried to kill me. We already have one murder — "

" — but no proof," protested Pomerance.

Ford placed his hands on the Counselor's desk and leaned into the man's face. "On the contrary, the crime is indisputable."

"And you suspect me . . ?"

"I suspect no one — yet. Finding the perp, that's the next step."

"You are tearing our social fabric to shreds."

"That's possible, it's already pretty damn threadbare."

He extended a hand toward the multiprobe in Pomerance's lap, inviting its return.

"This could get much worse, Counselor. Wouldn't you like me to make a call — keep the Marines in their barracks?"

Pomerance let out a weary sigh and handed the multiprobe back to its rightful owner without a word.

▼

A few minutes later, in the privacy of Rooney's apartment, Ford configured his multiprobe for an important call:

> *BlueTalk — Agent Blue Eyes reporting freedom of action regained. Maintain expeditionary force readiness, but do not launch. Stand down for now. Repeat, stand down.*

STEP FIVE

41

THE PASSWORD PAGE from the document archive discovered by Thuvia Lofgren was enigmatic. No annotations to reveal what each peculiar text string was good for.

On this morning in the Town Hall, Ford and Hoberman were coaxing the Town Manager to show them what Motro, the baseball throwing industrial robot, had been up to when P.L. Scott was killed.

"Come on, Tammy, there's gotta be a log of Motro's movements," insisted Ford.

"Such a log may or may not exist," returned the Town Manager. She was wearing a suit and tie today and speaking from behind a virtual executive desk. Her hands were folded to indicate her indifference to human concerns. "But if it does, it is password protected."

"We've tried every one on the page."

"You could try different search terms," she suggested with a patronizing grin. "Or, possibly a combination of passwords. Some of my classified files are very demanding."

Hoberman did some math. "We have a dozen passwords listed. If we take them in permutations of two, without repetition, but order matters, there are sixty-six possibilities."

"We'll be here all year," groaned Ford.

"Yes."

Ford looked over the password page,

"Maybe not, Nilo — one of the words contains $R1,$ and another one — look here — shows $R2$ right in the middle there."

"Hmm," said Hoberman, and passed along their choices.

Tammy smiled a cruel smile when the plan didn't work.

"Very good guess, gentlemen, but that combination will not unlock my logs or anything else, I'm sorry to say."

Ford shook his head. "You don't sound very sorry, old girl."

Tammy shrugged. "I know. I just says things like that because I like you guys."

Undaunted by Tammy's condescending tone, Ford and Hoberman went back to work, and two hours later they offered this pair of passwords on combination twenty-one . . .

KEY-H1-users

QZ-237-FAv50

. . . and the lock clicked . . . *whew.*

Tammy now appeared as an auto repair mechanic in striped coveralls and goggles.

"Congratulations, boys. Now pay attention: among the logs pertaining to machinery, I have fifteen rovers and five robots. What's your pleasure?"

"Motro," said Ford. "Six months ago. Coordinate with the time of P.L. Scott's death."

"Scott died on twenty-one April, Mars Year Thirty-Seven. Fetching Motro log that date."

Ford inched closer to the screen. "And, we need all the video surveillance records for the same period. To coordinate, you know."

"Well . . . they're private. Personal data, et cetera." Tammy tilted her head, confused momentarily by the need to make a delicate decision.

Hoberman got the message. "Hey, Tam, we're not looking for citizens doing whatever they might be doing. Our focus is Motro."

"He's a robot, not a citizen . . ." interjected Ford.

Hoberman nodded. "And the video recordings are really part of the Motro log. Watch the movements we're checking. Big help to us."

The Town Manager seemed to consider the request. Ford and Hoberman were getting ready to cross their fingers when Tammy pointed to the Township computer they were using.

"Place a static storage device in Tray Six, please."

Hoberman dropped a penny-sized disc into the tray.

"Transferring Motro log file and pertinent video surveillance for twenty-one April, Mars Year Thirty-Seven."

"Thanks, Tammy," exclaimed Ford.

"Do not mention it — do not — no mention — none," said she.

▼

In their little office adjoining the rover shop, Ford and Hoberman tried to make sense of Motro's movements on the day of P.L. Scott's murder.

"Well, shit," he griped, "I see a lot of numbers — they look like directions, distance traveled, turns, stops, starts, you name it — but I can't put a sequence together that makes any sense."

Hoberman was pessimistic. "Maybe we got ourselves what you Earthers call a *bum steer*. Not the key after all."

Ford thought he detected a shifty attitude behind the words.

"You okay, Nilo? We know Motro was involved. Here's what I do see — a joystick controller ID."

"Yeah, I see that."

"And it's Motro's controller, the one I was using when we fired him up, and the ID I'm currently working with."

Hoberman shifted his weight. "Lot of joysticks in The Ark — every kid has one. But let's see here . . . registered to Motro . . ." He scanned through Motro's logfile, a long and boring search. Then, embedded the middle of the header block, he spotted a cryptic sequence of characters:

#&@*PJ$!>>JS-A4<<%@B7Q6#$

"Um, try *JS-A4.* "

Ford was perplexed. "How do I switch controllers?"

"You don't," grunted Hoberman. "I've got this." He scrolled the logfile text back to the beginning. With the press of a key he called forth a dialog box, typed *J - S – A - 4,* and clicked on the *OK* button.

A window opened on Ford's computer screen showing the hulking industrial robot in Central Park as seen from a wall-mounted surveillance camera.

"Motro," said Hoberman. "Over there across the park."

Ford squinted at the image. "Not much detail from here, but look — someone is bent over at the edge of the lake."

"P.L. Scott?"

"Not sure."

"What is he doing?"

"Don't know. Pulling weeds?"

"How to scroll forward?"

"Right arrow."

"Got it."

Ford pressed the arrow key and the video advanced in real time. Motro suddenly came to life. He swiveled toward the man busy at the lake's edge and moved slowly toward him.

"Uh-oh"

Both of Motro's clawed arms extended outward. They took the man in a steely grip and thrust him headfirst into the lake. The man's arms and legs thrashed and kicked for almost a minute. Then they went limp.

"Jesus."

"Stop here."

Hoberman reached across the keyboard and hit the escape key.

"We've got this recorded, right?" asked Ford. "Tammy can't erase it?"

"Yeah, it's here on my disc. Evidence, huh?"

"The very best kind. Let's see what else we've got."

Ford pressed the arrow key. They watched Motro hoist the man, now a corpse, out of the water, turn, and trundle away toward the western park exit.

"Fast forward."

Hoberman tapped the arrow key twice. The scene shifted to the South Prom. Motro approached and passed under the surveillance camera with the man's body firmly in his grip. Now Ford and Hoberman had a good look at the dead man's face.

"P.L. Scott, you think?"

Hoberman nodded slowly. "I met the guy a few times. That's him. Was anyway."

"Amazing how the Prom is deserted. No witnesses."

"It's early, everyone's asleep."

The time hack in one corner of the video feed showed the hour: *6:05 AM.*

"And Brother Scott is sleeping forever," lamented Ford. "Fast forward again."

They watched the lumbering Motro seem to speed down the empty thoroughfare, bump a switch that opened an airlock, and exit into the West Side Auxiliary corridor.

"Slow now."

Once Motro was inside, a surveillance camera mounted over the exit to the far airlock picked up the corpse-laden robot as it advanced along the corridor and then halted midway. Motro's arms slowly drooped, his claws opened, and P.L. Scott's body slumped onto the corridor floor.

Motro turned ninety degrees. His scoop-like arm rotated

upward into view. It tilted forward, then back. A baseball — just a blur — exploded skyward and punched a hole in the polycarbonate roof.

"That's some meteor strike, Nilo," said Ford.

Hoberman cringed. "Yup."

Motro turned the other way. His scoop tilted forward, and a another baseball shot out. It gouged the flooring and ricocheted around the corridor. Motro wheeled over to its final resting place. There a hose-like appendage emerged from his right claw and swallowed the ball.

Ford and his apprentice scanned through the remaining video feed to see Motro safely back in his lakeside position, and no citizen the wiser for his murderous actions.

▼

"Make a duplicate of this stuff," ordered the PSA agent.

Hoberman copied the incriminating information from one disc to another.

Ford reached out. "Now hand it over."

Hoberman obliged. He couldn't help but notice the deep frown cleaving Ford's brow. "What? What's wrong?"

Ford tossed the tiny disc into the air like flipping a coin. Once twice, a dozen times. Hoberman watched it uneasily.

"Motro is a killer," declared Ford, "the instrument of murder, but not himself a murderer. Some unknown human being was running him. Apparently doing so with a secondary robot controller designated JS-A4."

"Looks that way," gulped Hoberman.

"Would that unknown human being be *you?*"

Hoberman flinched. "No sir."

Ford pointed a finger. "You were involved, though, of that I have no doubt. Tell me how."

"I'm not sure I know what you mean. I didn't kill anybody."

"Someone had to set up the secondary controller. Clearly you knew all about it — you set it up again today for us."

"Mmm . . ."

"Just as clearly, you set it up for the owner of joystick JS-A4."

"Oh no . . ."

"The question is — who owns that joystick? Lycus? Ismenius?"

"Um . . ."

Ford leaned toward Hoberman, his lips pursed in disgust. "No? Then who?"

Hoberman's face went white. "I . . . I can't tell you. I'm sworn, sworn to secrecy."

Ford absorbed the protest with a sardonic nod.

"Okay, if that's the case, I think I know everything I need to know without another word."

42

THE OWNER of the joystick designated JS-A4 was not a mystery to the Town Manager when Joe Ford made an inquiry, nor was the information classified, as he feared it might be.

"Thank you, Tammy. Important development. You may have solved a crime."

"Crime, Brother Ford? What's that?"

"When someone does something against the law."

Tammy was confused. "We don't have laws in the Independent Republic of Mars. We don't need them."

"Violating a recognized standard of conduct then, how's that?"

"The Like Minded have their faith, not standards."

"Well, even the Like Minded can't just kill anyone."

"Kill? You mean cut power, turn someone off?"

"In a manner of speaking, yes."

"But that's not so bad. I've been turned off, and I came right back on when power was restored."

Ford gave the Town Manager's naïve avatar a wry smile. "Who loaded your general knowledge file, Tam? Whoever that guy was, he missed some details. Human beings can't be turned back on when they're dead."

"Too bad. You organics, all imperfect."

"Yup."

▼

Ford was on his way from the Town Hall to the Town Media Studio, where he hoped to find Thuvia Lofgren, when he heard loud voices echoing around a nearby corner on East Central Boulevard. He paused to listen. A few seconds working to decode the cacophony told him that trouble was brewing. He rounded the corner and there discovered an angry mob shouting insults and threatening bodily harm to Active Deacon Lycus Salazar.

"Toady! Fool! Thug! Now we've got you!"

Salazar raised his arms. "I order you to disperse. The Like Minded must live in harmony."

"Harmony! Thought! Try *action,* pal!"

The nearest man barged forward and delivered a body block that slammed Salazar into the corridor wall. The Deacon managed to regain his balance, but another angry mobster shot out an elbow, dropping hm to his knees.

"That for your fucking social contract!"

"Right! Tell your Counselor — his days of religious tyranny are over!"

Someone kicked Salazar in the ribs, knocking him flat.

"Uhhh . . ."

Ford had heard enough. He clawed his way through the crowd and took up a position in front of Salazar to protect him from further mayhem. Undeterred, the mob surged forward.

"Stop where you are," Ford commanded.

He hefted his multiprobe, pressed a combination of buttons and waved the device, now humming dangerously, in the mob's red faces.

"Out of the way, Earther!" yelled the nearest man, evidently the ringleader.

"One more step and . . ."

". . . and what? You'll test our circuits?"

That got a laugh.

Ford shoved his multiprobe into the man's chest and squeezed its handle.

zzapp

Down went the man, rolling in agony.

The mob stumbled to a halt. Its members jostled each other uncertainly. Those in front were wary; those behind were pushing and shoving to press their cause. Growls and grumbles filled the air.

"Anyone else?" queried Ford.

The mob's unity of purpose drained away. The anger subsided as quickly as it flamed up.

"Get out of here," he ordered.

The mobsters turned this way and that, whining and complaining.

"But before you go — what got you so excited?"

The ringleader dragged himself erect. "There's been a murder. Yes? That's what we hear. What if we have another one? We're not safe anymore."

"The settlement isn't a war zone," countered Ford.

"The Town Charter is explicit — we need to start a government — but these spineless custodians won't act."

"That may change," said Ford. "Now scram" — he waved his multiprobe at the gathering — "before I lose my temper."

With many a whimper, the mobsters drifted away.

Ford leaned over and helped Salazar to his feet.

"You going to be okay?"

Salazar nodded ruefully. "No problem."

"You sure? You look kind of dazed."

Salazar swallowed. "Those eyes, those faces. I've never seen such rage. Who knew we were so hated?"

"Welcome to reality, Liko. Humanity in full flower."

▼

Ford did not find Lofgren in the Media Studio offices. Instead he ran into Zoran Boskovoy, who was preparing a formal paper on his science findings.

"Hey, Joe, look here," enthused Boskovoy, jabbing a finger at an esoteric diagram on his computer screen, "I've been crunching the data, and remember that old relic of a telescope you fixed up?"

Ford winced. "How can I forget?"

"It has most definitely detected *at least one planet* orbiting HD162826, like I suspected. Maybe more than one."

That's great, Zoran. Seen Thuvia?"

Boskovoy rolled his chair away from his desk. He scratched his head. "Not a chance. She won't see me, talk to me, have anything to do with me."

Ford opened up his handheld and made a call.

"Nilo? Where's your best girl hiding out today?"

Pause.

"Unh-huh, okay, got it."

He ended the call and turned to leave.

Boskovoy stood up. "You found Thuvia? Know where she is?"

Ford shrugged.

"You're on your way there. Mind if I tag along?"

Ford shook his head. "Not a good idea, Zo."

Boskovoy slumped back into his chair. "Well then, tell her — tell her I just want to talk. Settle things."

"Will do."

Ford started for the door again, then turned back. "So . . . let me get this straight . . . you found a planet circling the Sun's long lost cousin. You think we've got cousins of our own living out there?"

"Who knows? Could be."

"Let's hope they're not as screwed up as we are."

▼

Ford scanned foot traffic on Interplanetary Highway to be sure he wasn't being tailed, let a few citizens pass him by, then cranked open the door of the East End Radio Antenna tower. There he found Thuvia Lofgren squatting on the floor behind the ladder, typing away on her laptop. Her ears were covered with headphones, and she was rocking to a beat only she could hear.

Ford knocked on the inside wall to get her attention without causing a heart attack.

"Ooh!" she squeaked, ripping off her headphones. "Joe! Shit! Startled me!"

Ford held up his tiny data storage button between thumb and forefinger. "Got a tray that can read this thing?"

Lofgren pointed to a blank area on her keyboard. Ford passed her the button.

"What is this?" she wondered.

Ford pointed at her screen. "Evidence of a murder. I need a slideshow, and you, Sister Lofgren, know how to make one."

Lofgren blanched. "There's a rumor going around. So it's true, huh? Someone got rubbed out."

"Rubbed out? You've been reading too many crime novels. Drowned, actually, as you will see."

"Geez, who? That guy Scott?"

"You know your gossip. Start with the man's manifesto" — he passed her a paper copy — "then give me the opening video and the final shot where the body gets dumped. Can do?"

"Of course."

Ford ran through other video clips he had loaded onto the storage button while Lofgren took notes. A long discussion followed. When they had the format thrashed out in detail he handed her a second slip of paper.

"Then add this text."

Lofgren examined Ford's scribbles. *"Oh! My! God!* This is the biggest story in history. *I'm drooling."*

4

Ford gave the young journalist a wan smile. "Biggest in the history of Cratertown anyway" — he pointed a warning finger at her — "I'm trusting you. No writing, no talking, no podcasts, not until the colony meets to discuss the situation."

Lofgren bobbed her head. "Yeah, I know. Scout's honor."

43

DID YOU HEAR? *Murder.* Murder right here in the habitat."

"Who?"

"That guy Scott . . . died a while back, and now they say he was killed."

"Who killed him?"

"One of us, can you believe?"

"I heard it was that big blue robot."

"Yeah? I heard it was his wife, Hesperia D. On account of he strayed too far from home."

"If she had it in her, which I doubt. I'm just saying, watch yourself around that bot."

The rumor mill was going strong at dinnertime in the Main Street Food Hall. The idea of an actual crime was so exotic and so delicious that the news-starved citizens of The Ark could talk of nothing else.

Except: the idea of government also stirred their blood. In the middle evening, Buster Mayfield stuck a crude handcrafted poster on the wall:

GET GOVERNMENT NOW
LET YOUR VOICE BE HEARD

"Time to stand up and be counted," he bellowed. "Throw off Like-Minded tyranny!"

"Tyranny is it?" came a contending voice, followed by a slab of lasagna hurled against the poster that splattered tomato sauce all over Mayfield.

Mayfield's allies were outraged. They fired back with potatoes and eggplants. The Like-Minded group fell back toward the kitchen, where they tipped over a table and continued their artillery barrage from behind the improvised fort.

Soon bottles and plates were flying through the air, launched from both sides. One of the men in the pro-government group rushed the Like-Minded position. The defenders knocked him flat. Oaths and curses filled the air. Punches were thrown.

Zoran Boskovoy was trying to eat a solitary meal in a far corner of the hall when the fighting broke out. He waded through the angry mob and took up a position at Mayfield's side, waving his hands like a football referee.

"Stop this stupid fight," he yelled. "Buster's got a point, and you're wasting our food."

His efforts were rewarded with a smear of lasagna and a potato that ricocheted off his head. He staggered and attempted to retreat. But someone with good aim pitched a coffee cup that caught him on his jaw, and down he went.

Buster Mayfield lifted Boskovoy from the floor, laced an arm under Boskovoy's waist, draped Boskovoy's right arm over his own shoulder, and dragged him out of the Hall.

▼

Dr. Rooney heard about the commotion while she was walking home. "Fighting in the Food Hall!" shouted a man running past her. He was covered with table scraps.

She rushed back to her infirmary, previously locked for the night, and re-opened for business.

She didn't have long to wait. Mayfield arrived with the semi-conscious Boskovoy hanging on his shoulder. He eased the wounded man onto an infirmary bed and bade the doctor goodnight.

"I'm a target myself, and I don't want the fight to spread over this way," he explained.

"Hey, Doc, how'm I doing . . ?" mumbled Boskovoy when Mayfield was gone, and his senses were reconnecting.

"You'll live," said Rooney, with ill-disguised scorn.

She examined the lump on his head and the purple bruise spreading across one cheek. She pressed fingers against his jaw.

"That hurt?"

"Uhhh . . ." he replied, twisting his head away.

She felt around the injury with a more delicate touch. "You've got a contusion, maybe a bone bruise. But your jaw isn't broken."

She pried his mouth open and felt his teeth.

"Teeth all good. What the hell is going on in the Food Hall?"

Boskovoy rolled his eyes.

"And, Jesus, Zoran, how did a sensible guy like you get himself involved?"

Boskovoy tried to sit up. Rooney gently pushed him back down on the bed.

"Easy there, Champ."

"Um, some of us" — he swallowed, started again — "citizens, a pretty good group . . . want to change how we live. The religious nuts were picking on Buster . . ."

"And you stood up for him?"

"I guess so, yeah, I did."

"That calm the crowd?" she asked with a skeptical grin.

"Hah — they're still at it, far as I know."

Rooney leaned over and kissed the bump on Boskovoy's head.

"My God, does Mars' biggest jerk secretly have principles?"

She inserted painkilling tablets into his aching mouth and made him swallow some water. She pulled a coverlet over him and sat down on a corner of the bed to await the wave of injured combatants she expected to come stumbling into her care.

44

THE STATISTICS were grim. Lycus Salazar stood before Ismenius Pomerance in the Counselor's office and recited the litany from notes he had written down on his handheld.

"Broken bones, zero. That's the good news. Injuries needing other emergency treatment at the infirmary, twenty-five.

"Property damage, like food service, plates and so forth — also chairs, tables, plus wall repair and paint — Imowelo estimates the cost at a couple thousand maroons. Much of the equipment will have to be reprinted, so this will take two weeks."

Pomerance scribbled some notes of his own.

"Two weeks? Right. That means a month. You say Mayfield started this?"

"He was the catalyst, but the tension was already there, and Boskovoy ignited the skirmish."

"God on High. I will think on this ugly matter, have some advice for the Deacons and our Founder by tomorrow."

He waved Salazar toward the door. "Action in Harmony."

"Harmony in Thought," replied Salazar, stepping out into the corridor.

"And Thought in Action," intoned Pomerance, completing the threefold mantra with a heavy sigh. His eyes fell to his notes, and he studied to make sense of them.

"Counselor?" Salazar had not gone far and was now sticking his head around Pomerance's open office door. "That guy Ford is here to see you. Should I let him in?"

Pomerance groaned and nodded.

Ford entered, closed the door to be sure they were alone, and stood behind the visitor's chair.

"We have our murderer," he announced.

Pomerance leaned back in his chair and spread his hands out.

"You here to arrest me?"

"Not at all, Counselor. I'm sure you weren't involved."

Pomerance leaned forward, suddenly curious about Ford's persistent bullshit. "Then who, pray tell?"

Ford produced a sheet of paper and held it up so Pomerance could read it. "What you see here on this page is the Town Manager's assignment of a certain joystick's ownership. You know, like the kind all the kids use to play video games."

Pomerance screwed up his mouth. "I see it. Joystick ID JS-A4."

"That's right."

"Your point?"

"The user of that joystick was in control of the industrial robot Motro when Motro drowned P.L. Scott in the Central Park lake, carried his body into the West Side Auxiliary corridor, and fired a baseball through the roof to make it look like Scott asphyxiated there."

Pomerance snatched the piece of paper from Ford's hand and crumpled it into a ball.

"You're good, Brother Ford. You restore our broken parts while you break our social structure."

"Motro is not a sentient being, Counselor."

Pomerance buried his head in his hands. "I don't begrudge the facts you've presented, grim as they are. But the Like Minded will not give up their ideals."

"Come on, Counselor — you know all about the unrest, the fights, the need to suppress dissent. I didn't cause any of it. I believe your charter is clear — if a felony crime occurs, you must declare a government."

Pomerance shook his head. "I wouldn't know how to go about

doing it. The charter is not available. Tammy no longer has a copy in her memory banks, if she ever did."

Ford raised a finger.

"I think some clever Like-Minded soul — a fanatic — made an erasure, possibly long ago. But I have someone standing by who can help you."

"Who's that?"

"An inquisitive young woman you may have met." Ford reached out and reopened the Counselor's office door. "Hey out there."

Thuvia Lofgren timidly appeared in the doorway. She was cradling a thick stack of paper in her arms.

"Hello, young lady, indeed, I think we have met. An interview for one of your podcasts, I believe. What have you got there?"

Lofgren deposited the paper stack on the Counselor's desk.

"This is the Settlement Charter," she proudly declared. "The original, not a copy."

"My goodness, where did you find it?"

"In a warehouse closet, out behind the Media Studio, sitting on a shelf along with a pile of plans and a whole list of passwords. I bet I'm the only person in that room since construction began."

Pomerance donned reading glasses and leafed through the pages."

"Well," he said. "Well, well, well."

45

DURING THE MORNING rush hour public display screens located above the airlocks and habitat doorways lit up with an unexpected message to citizens of The Ark:

ALL HANDS MEETING
12:00 SHARP TODAY
AGENDA: SETTLEMENT STATUS
PLAN TO ATTEND

A little-used module adjoining Central Park was dedicated to religious services, concerts, plays, and old movies. It could seat five hundred people, the entire population of The Ark, and it was the designated venue for that rarity of rarities, a town meeting.

Citizens started lining up for the occasion soon after breakfast. Active Deacons opened the doors at 11:30.

By 12:00 noon, more than a hundred and fifty people had been seated (in folding chairs crafted by Hesperia Dale).

At 12:05, Ismenius Pomerance strode to the front of the room lugging the Settlement Charter in a vinyl carry bag. He stepped onto a low stage, crossed to a chest-high podium, and there surveyed the crowd with a practiced eye, looking for hostility carried over from recent events, finding only curiosity. True, the crowd wasn't quite as big as he had expected, but he was used to citizen indifference, which he imagined helped people ignore their problems and embrace their possibilities.

"Hello, everyone — who loves the Independent Republic of Mars?"

A roar of assent went up from the assembly.

"All right. Count me in. And who loves The Ark, our home?"

Another roar, a hearty cheer, vibrated through the hall.

"Good to hear, because our business today will test your love."

Murmurs of confusion greeted this pronouncement.

"Why is that?" he asked rhetorically. "Because . . . I must report a crime." He took a nervous breath. "A *murder.*"

A collective gasp issued from his audience.

"Yes. You heard correctly. Six months ago, our dear friend P.L. Scott, long presumed dead from lack of air, was in fact murdered. Done in by someone in our midst, one of the Like Minded, as difficult as that is to understand."

Cries of wounded indignation erupted. Someone in the middle stood up, waving for recognition. "Who did this? Who is responsible?"

Ismenius raised a hand to calm the man down. "We'll get to that, I hope. Meanwhile . . ."

With a theatrical flourish, he removed the Settlement Charter from his bag and let it fall squarely onto the podium. The heavy thump the pages made on the polished slab could be heard all the way to the back row.

"The Ark was given a Charter when it started, many years ago, and this is it," he explained. "Acknowledging the ways and preferences of the Like Minded, it mandated that no government would be allowed to rule over us — "

" — No! No! Absolutely not!" came shouts of outrage.

"*Unless,*" continued Pomerance, "unless a crime was committed, and then we would agree to inaugurate formal rules, elect officers, set up courts, establish a police force."

"Never!" roared the crowd, starting to get hot.

"Hang on, everyone. As children mature, they outgrow their clothes, and as our settlement has matured, so have we outgrown our casual ways."

By now every citizen was standing, shouting objections.

Pomerance gripped the stack of paper he had brought to the meeting and held it aloft. "Our Charter is specific on this point," he insisted. "There is no room for argument. And today it is our job to elect our first President, who will then begin the process of organizing our lives."

A wave of irate citizens surged toward the podium. "Hand over that pile of crap! Burn it! We don't need any charter!"

"Oh yes, we do," countered a small group led by Nilo Hoberman that elbowed themselves into a protective ring around the podium.

The two factions pushed and shoved each other. Someone lifted one of Dale's chairs and brought it down on the young Active Deacon. He turned in time to take the blow on his back, but the impact drove him to the floor.

"STOP THIS NONSENSE!" boomed an artificially amplified voice. The skirmishers paused as Hadley Timmerman, The Ark's Founder, rolled into the room in his high-tech wheelchair. They saluted, bowed, and parted to let the old man motor to the front of the hall, where he pivoted around to address them.

"Murder!" he thundered. "Yes, and who is the murderer? Who among us dared to murder our society along with that man Scott?"

"Who? Who?" chorused the mob.

"I'll tell you who — someone without scruples, someone who knew how to bend our systems to his evil purpose."

"Tell us! Name the bastard! *Name the name!*"

The Founder turned his chair around. He pointed at the fallen Deacon. "Here you have him — a traitor to us all — Nilosyrtis Hoberman."

Hoberman's supporters lifted him up and dusted him off. He wobbled backward to evade the opposition clawing at his throat.

Joe Ford had seen all he wanted to see. He worked his way through the mob and climbed onto the stage beside Counselor Pomerance, who was reeling in shock.

"Hey there!" he shouted. "We're citizens here, not animals! Calm down! Down! Down! *Down, already!*"

The actual fighting eased up, but the howls of angry resentment did not.

Ford stuck fingers into his mouth and let forth an earsplitting whistle. That got everyone's attention.

"Okay, then. Here's what I know — Hoberman is innocent."

The crowd grumbled their disappointment, but their shouts and curses faded away.

"Let me show you something."

He held up a tiny storage button for all to see, dropped it into the podium computer's data reader, and pressed a switch. Behind him, a wall-size display screen came to life.

"Let's start with *motive* — why would anyone want to kill P.L. Scott?"

The first slide in the deck created by Thuvia Lofgren showed Scott's manifesto advocating political change.

"Well, this looks like a serious challenge to the way things work around here. Revolutionary ideas, and dangerous to those in charge."

He pressed a key and a photo of the robot Motro appeared.

"Next, *means* — how did it happen? The video you're about to see will be disturbing, so fasten your seatbelts."

He pressed another key and Motro came to life in the video that captured him drowning Scott.

The assembly reacted with horrified gasps and groans.

"Sorry to put you through this, but it's important that you all see for yourselves — Scott really was murdered. A terrible crime has been committed."

He brought up a slide showing a few lines of Motro's movement log with the joystick JS-A4 highlighted.

"Finally, *opportunity* — Let's see who was controlling poor dumb Motro. Normally, he is operated by a joystick stored right there in his body, a device bearing the digital ID *MJ-1A*. I've used it myself. But in this instance, control was switched to a different device, *JS-A4*. Where is that joystick? Who does it belong to?"

By now the assembled citizens were paying close attention to Ford's evidence and his argument.

Ford pointed at the image. "What do you think?"

Murmurs of speculation stirred the attendees. The question was already on everyone's lips.

"Well, folks, that joystick is right here in this room. It is permanently attached to our Founder's wheelchair. And here we have the murderer himself sitting in that chair — Hadley Timmerman."

An outpouring of astonishment and cries of betrayal flooded the room, cut short by the accused, who turned away from the screen to address the crowd.

"THIS IS RIDICULOUS," the old man protested at maximum volume. "TRAITOROUS SLANDER."

He thumbed his incriminating joystick, and his wheelchair rolled him away to the exit.

THIS IS NOTHING BUT A REVOLUTIONARY PLOT AND I WON"T LISTEN TO ANOTHER LYING WORD."

▼

In the protective confines of his residence, the Founder called for an Active Deacon, and Lycus Salazar duly appeared.

"Sir?"

"Help me get my suit on, Liko. There's a good man."

Salazar fetched the Founder's pressure suit, and struggling mightily, managed to wrap the old man up in it.

"What's the occasion?" he asked, straining to pull the suit over the Founder's chairbound torso. "I can't remember the last time you ventured outside."

"I've let things slip, and I believe it's time to inspect the eastern perimeter. You know" — he checked his watch — "Deimos will be visible this afternoon. Always like to get a view. Helmet?"

Salazar handed him his helmet. "Got your rad tag?"

"Right here on the dashboard. But I won't need it, I've been edited."

Salazar zipped up the suit. "Oxygen? Battery charge?"

The Founder smiled. "All topped up, son. Thanks for taking good care of me."

With that he motored away, out of his door, and then ten blocks along Interplanetary Highway to the East Sally Port Airlock.

He donned his helmet and clicked a switch on his chair. The airlock doors opened and he taxied in.

Moments later he was out on the hostile surface of Mars, unprotected by manmade structures.

"Ahh," he said, "the wide open spaces. *Yippee-ki-yay.*"

Deimos, Mars' lesser moon, seemed to hover over the eastern horizon. He aimed his wheelchair in its direction. The chair's tires bit into the crater sand and he rolled toward it, rolled for miles.

▼

PODCAST HOST:

Hey, it's Thuvia, *The Real Maid of Mars,* back on the air with some shocking news. Turns out, the Founder of our settlement committed a *murder.* Can you believe that? Now our whole social system is in a whirl. I caught up with our first President — that's right, we're getting organized — with some big questions. Sad day? Happy day? Which is it, sir?

POMERANCE:

Both, I guess. Happy that everyone is calming down. Sad that our Founder has passed away.

PODCAST HOST:

Tell us what happened.

POMERANCE:

He put on a suit and drove until his air ran out.

PODCAST HOST:

Hard to think about that. But now you got voted in . . .

POMERANCE:

Partly thanks to you and the Charter you found, young lady.

PODCAST HOST:

. . . so what's next?

POMERANCE:

Elect a council and set the date for another election. I'm just a caretaker.

PODCAST HOST:

I guess we may not be saying *Brother* or *Sister* anymore. Thank you for talking with me, *Mister* President.

And now let's hear from Joe Ford, the man who turned us upside down. Do you feel responsible for the Founder's death?

FORD:

Whoa, Thuvia, you're starting to sound like a real journalist. Answer is, no, I don't.

PODCAST HOST:

Think his suicide means he was guilty?

FORD:

I do. I was pretty sure it was him using the joystick on his cart, and now we know.

PODCAST HOST:

What about his assistants, the Deacons?

FORD:

Well, Nilo is an accessory. He helped the Founder do his dirty work. But he didn't know it would lead to murder, and he confessed, so we're forgiving him. Lycus Salazar, on the other hand, was too close to the old man, too sympathetic to trust. We don't have courts yet or any kind of brig, so we're doing what the Brits used to do —

transport criminals to far away places. In our case, that's a first-class ticket to Big Blue.

PODCAST HOST:
And yourself? Crime solved, you going back?

FORD:
I'm thinking about it.

46

THAT DREAM, it was happening again. At irregular intervals, usually just before the dawn of a new day, Ford became trapped in a stretch of his former life on Earth, dressed in combat gear, an army officer leading a small squad of loyal North American soldiers against the *Divisor* uprising. On this morning he found himself hiking across an arid upland, avoiding the enemy's explosive drones by duckling under gnarly juniper trees. Then, high on a mountainside with an opposition outpost in the sights of his aerodart launcher, he became airborne, tossed high by the shock wave of an incoming artillery shell. He came down in jail.

He reached out to touch the cool adobe walls, tested the wrought iron bars, and recoiled from the *Divisor carcelero,* who advanced with a stiletto ready to stab.

But no, the stiletto was a key. The *carcelero* swung the cell bars wide and made a sweeping gesture toward an open doorway. Ford turned toward the snowclad peaks framed within.

As he moved past the *carcelero* to make his exit, the man turned into a woman; a woman who, although clad in military fatigues, looked a lot like Dana Rooney.

"This way," she said.

Ford passed through the door and started along a winding mountain path under a bright blue sky. His feet were crunching on thin layers of icy snow until, without warning, the landscape became a cold and trackless desert. A small moon was moving overhead. The Sun, made hazy by a veil of dust, failed to dispel the chill.

"Ahhh — !"

A hand pushed against his shoulder.

"Jesus, Joe. Wake up."

Ford abruptly sat up and looked around. Curled up beside him was Dr. Rooney. No dream.

"God, where was I?" he groaned.

"The war again?" she asked in a sleepy voice.

"Maybe. Jail for sure, adobe walls . . . something else . . ."

"What?"

"Something different . . . I don't know exactly."

"Come on, while the memory is fresh."

"Someone . . . did . . . *something* . . . I don't know what."

He swung his feet onto the floor.

"I better get up. Lots to do."

Rooney took his hand and kissed it. He leaned back over her and returned the favor before scrambling free and heading for an always brief shower.

▼

The Ark took pride in having a commercial district as useful and attractive as any small town on Earth. A string of bodegas with clever signage fronted North Axis Promenade, luring customers for clothes, snacks, toys, trinkets, and all kinds of household goods. Many of the items on sale were imported at great cost from Earth. Others were handcrafted by locals or recycled from a succession of previous owners.

The Mars Mart sold jewelry.

No one was manning the counter when Ford arrived. He touched a buzzer and an employee appeared from behind a curtain.

"Good morning, Joe," said Hesperia Dale.

Ford made an elaborate show of surprise by bringing his hands up against his face.

"Hesper, what are you doing here?"

She smiled. "I'm one of the owners. And an occasional salesperson. See the pins and necklaces in the case here?"

Ford bent down to examine the exquisite titanium and gold creations.

"Yours?"

"Of course."

Ford immediately felt very uncomfortable, but he had nowhere else to go.

"I want to buy a diamond," he croaked. "You know, a Martian one. What have you got?"

Dale studied her ex with suspicious eyes. "Well, as it happens, I do have a few."

She lifted a velvet-lined tray from the display case. Several yellow diamonds glittered attractively under the overhead lights.

"As you may or may not know, subtle inclusions of nitrogen and potassium prove where they came from. Their provenance. The elemental isotopes are different from Earthly gems."

Ford swallowed. "Make it a small one — money is not unlimited."

Dale used a pair of plastic tongs to pick up a likely candidate.

"This might work. One-tenth caret."

"It's beautiful. How much?"

"Five hundred maroons."

Ford exhaled explosively. The regal sum felt like a punch in the stomach.

"Woof."

He waggled his head uncertainly. Then: "Okay, I'll take it."

"Bravo."

Ford took another look at the jewelry on display.

"I know you do a lot of 3-D printing. Can you make a ring?"

Dale snorted. "Or help you find something. What about one of these?"

She showed off an array of rings in another velvet-lined tray.

"Take your pick."

Ford took his time looking over the merchandise, muttering to himself. At last his gaze settled on a gold band with vinelike tracery engraved on its circumference. Tiny claws were poised to grip his modest diamond.

"What do you think?"

She laughed. "Excellent choice, sir."

"When can I have it?"

"Hmm, someone's leaving town. Who's this for, I wonder."

Ford bit his lip.

"You're right, it's a gift. Settle a social debt."

Dale's face flushed red. "Sorry to probe. That was rude."

"Hey, no trouble. You made a nice ring."

▼

Later that day Dale sat in front of her computer and stared at the image of the replacement valve body she was working on. She didn't know what it was meant to do, only that she had already printed four prototypes, and they all leaked.

She moved her mouse around to rotate the virtual model while examining the smaller but solidly real counterpart that Ford had loaned her.

"There's no difference, just size and . . . clearance."

She sighed, stood up, and brewed herself a cup of coffee.

"Damn those plumbers," she complained.

Then she sat back down and added one-tenth of a millimeter to the diameter of the replacement valve body.

After printing it, she walked it out to the Farm and handed it off to Buster Mayfield, who plugged in a flexible irrigation hose and dialed up the pressure.

"Well, what do you know, girl . . . this one holds up."

Indeed, no leak whatsoever. But water pressure blew the valve ten meters into the trees, and it took Dale and Mayfield half an hour to find it.

47

THE RING IS READY," read the message on Joe Ford's handheld.

He returned to the Mars Mart on slow feet, feeling shy about another encounter with his estranged wife, worried about her natural curiosity, repelled by her often sharp tongue, anxious to avoid adding to a long string of misunderstandings.

"Morning, Hesper. Got your text," he said.

Dale nodded, disappeared for a moment into her tiny stockroom behind the shop's curtain, and reappeared carrying a large object wrapped in a towel.

"Here you go, Brother Ford, your order . . ."

Ford looked blank.

She grinned and unwrapped the object, which, no surprise, was not a ring.

"It's leakproof," she said.

"My valve!" exclaimed Ford. "Finally."

"Prototype Number Five. Let the water flow."

"I most certainly will see that it does. Under tight control, of course, thanks to you."

Dale reached into a drawer and removed a jeweler's polishing cloth, folded in half. She placed it on the counter and, with a merchant's keen presentation sense, gently lifted one edge to reveal the gold band Ford had picked out, already a handsome thing, now made dazzling by a tiny claw-mounted yellow diamond.

"Ooh," said Ford.

"Yup," returned Dale, proud of her work.

Ford picked it up and would have simply stuffed it in a shirt pocket, but Dale grabbed his hand. "No, no, let me box it."

She brought forth a box made of faux wood and placed the ring inside with loving care.

"Five hundred maroons."

Ford showed his handheld to Dale's countertop paybot, resigning himself to short rations for the next week.

She handed him the box with a wistful look on her face. "Take care of yourself back on Big Blue."

Ford shrugged. *"Que sera,* you know?"

▼

Interplanetary Cycler-02, one of three ships in regular rotation between Earth and Mars, was just a few days out from Phobos Station on its outbound run, and Ford was helping Dr. Rooney pack up for her long-awaited return to the mother world. In five year's residency she had accumulated a lot of stuff.

"I could leave the clothes," she mused. "I'll be sleeping on the cycler anyway, and I could hit New York hard for the latest threads. What do you think?"

Ford stopped packing. "Save some weight," he acknowledged.

She was warming to her subject. "And I wouldn't mind a real shopping spree."

Ford scowled. "In fancy stores. Take in a play on Broadway."

"Damn right."

Ford gestured at the duffle he was cramming full of sweaters and blouses. "So, do I pack your gear or not?"

Rooney's anticipatory grin gave way to a sour look. She folded her arms. "All right, Joe, what's bothering you?"

"Nothing. New York? I've never been there."

"So? Out with it."

"I'm not going to New York."

"Okay . . . you don't have to."

"Or anywhere else on Earth."

Rooney's face turned pale. "Oh, Joe . . ."

She sat down on her bed with a thump. Her eyes flooded, and she remained there, immobilized by the bad news, for long minutes.

Ford didn't know what to say or do. Watching her slowly take in the meaning of it all caused an upwelling of guilt that made his cheeks burn. "You must have had some idea. This can't be a total surprise."

At last Rooney shook her head to clear it. "Maybe not, but I thought we really had something," she said.

Ford stuck his hands in his pockets. "We did," he said, then amended the thought. "We do. Always will."

"Oh yeah, from two hundred million kilometers."

Rooney stood up and began ramming clothes and knickknacks into her packs.

"It's Hesperia. Somehow, even though she's treated you like dirt, you can't shake her off. You love her?"

"I don't know," he confessed. "You're hot, she's cool, but the difference is we want the same kind of life, right here where we are."

"Gee whiz, Joe, that's not much to go on in this cramped little ghetto."

"Yeah, I'm taking a big chance . . ."

Rooney puckered her mouth and knitted her brows. Ford could see the gears turning inside her head. At last she nodded to some unvoiced decision. Her face hardened.

"All right, Brother Ford, at least see me off. We'll wave to each other."

48

ARK BUS ZERO THREE, the largest vehicle on the planet, was waiting in the Rover Shop for Earthbound passengers to board.

Zoran Boskovoy and Eridania Rooney stood near the observation room airlock while precious cylinders of heavy hydrogen and sealed boxes containing Martian diamonds were placed in the cargo bay. They were anticipating a smooth departure and the pleasures of open air back on Big Blue. Standing behind them with notably less enthusiasm was Lycus Salazar. He scanned the crowd of onlookers for support, saw only stony faces.

Thuvia Lofgren worked up her nerve and approached the man who had been hunting her.

"Hey, Zo — I want a full report from Earth when you get there. Photos — clothes, cars, newspaper headlines, everything."

Boskovoy was relieved to have his fruitless chase come to an end. "Sorry about what happened, Thoo. Now I get the chance to tell you what I would have told you from the get-go — you're free." He gently brushed fingers against her noticeably swollen belly. "I wouldn't dream of trapping you into some kind of ugly marriage."

Nilo Hoberman squeezed through the assembled well-wishers and took Lofgren's hand in his.

Boskovoy smiled. "Nilo — can't wait to see me off. You going to be Dad?"

Lofgren ran an arm around Hoberman's waist. "That has yet to be determined. We're negotiating."

Hoberman grudged a smile. "Let's see how it goes."

When the last of the cargo was safely stowed aboard the bus,

Ed Imowelo opened the airlock.

"All aboard for Planet Earth," he called out.

Salazar waved to the Active Deacons and stepped through the door.

Joe Ford shook Boskovoy's hand as he passed by and wrapped his arms around Rooney.

"So long, Doc."

"Happy trails. Avoid those killer sun flares."

She tilted her chin up, and the temporary lovers shared a brave farewell smooch that elicited whistles and catcalls from everyone except Hesperia Dale, who stumbled away from the humiliating moment with a grim red face.

After the travelers were out of sight and the airlock door had closed behind them, she remembered that she didn't notice whether Rooney was wearing a ring or not.

▼

The roof over The Ark's public works warehouse was the first one ever installed, thirty-odd Mars years ago, and it had recently been replaced for safety reasons. The new polycarbonate material extended downward to the ground on the side that faced east, the result of an architectural decision made when the settlement was new, and the designers worried about claustrophobia. The Sun's ultraviolet rays had yet to craze the plastic surface, and because the view took in the ferry hangar, an excited crowd of event-starved citizens had gathered there to watch the ferry itself depart for Phobos Station.

Hesperia Dale was there among the onlookers, as curious as the rest. And like the rest, she oohed and ahhed when the hangar doors opened wide.

The ferry emerged into hazy sunlight and taxied away out of view. The crowd held its breath. Then it reappeared, rolling fast in the opposite direction, tilting up and rising into the dusty sky on wide wings.

The crowd roared. A few minutes later, Dale spotted sunlight glinting off the hull, now high above, circling around in the thin atmosphere, spiraling up toward outer space.

As she tracked the ship zooming overhead, her eye was drawn away by the sight of Joe Ford standing nearby. He made no attempt to pretend he was watching the ferry.

"Oh shit," she said and motioned him to join her.

Ford ambled over. He smiled, said nothing.

"What are you doing here? I thought you'd be getting on that ship with Dana," said Dale.

Ford nodded. "I might have, but I didn't."

Dale pointed up at the ferry as it faded from view.

"Too late now."

Ford shrugged. "There'll be another ferry on another day."

"I suppose so," granted Dale.

"I won't be on that one either."

Dale took a half step back. She stared hard at Ford, weighing his words. Her eyes flashed. "You liked her."

"Yes I did. But she craves blue skies and big cities. I may not be the likest of the Like Minded, but I left Earth in the rear view mirror when I was taken prisoner down in New Mexico."

Dale breathed out a sigh of resignation.

"Well then, we ought to clean up the mess we've made."

49

APPOINTMENT REQUIRED," said the wide green door as Dale and Ford came into view. "Do you have one?"

"Yes. Ford and Dale here to see President Pomerance."

"Please wait."

Ford noted the carvings inlaid with gold leaf, now partly covered by a paper sign that read, *IRM Administration.*

The design is nice," observed Ford with a smile. "I wonder who the artist was."

"Do you? Well, if you don't know, the Founder was a very persuasive man. Hard to refuse a request, even when it violated all our rules."

Ford was about to agree when the door retracted into its side pocket.

"Appointment verified. Please come in," said the door.

The adoring photos of the Founder that had decorated the hallway on Ford's previous visits were gone, replaced by spartan white paint. Inside the opulent atrium, Ismenius Pomerance stood up from a bench beside the central pool to greet them. He was wearing a jacket and tie.

"Mister President," said Dale, making a respectful curtsy.

"Hello, Hesperia, Joseph."

"That's a new look for you, sir," said Ford.

Pomerance grinned and resumed his seat. "I'm new at this, so I'm trying to look the part. Here, sit with me."

The pair settled onto a bench facing the President. Trivium Quinn appeared with cold drinks.

"Quite a change from your old office," said Ford, sipping what tasted like mint tea.

"I'm learning hospitality. A political lesson, I'm told."

He fingered his tie.

"Trivium, who is now my administrative assistant, said you want to dissolve your marriage, am I right?"

Ford and Dale looked at each other.

"That's right," they chorused.

"And why is that?"

Dale shook her head. "The marriage has never worked. Too much suspicion."

"Our agendas got in the way," added Ford. "And we both want to move forward, get a new start."

"I see," said Pomerance. "In the old days, a week ago, I would have frowned upon encouraging single adults. But our new government is more tolerant. So be it."

He made a hand signal and Quinn reappeared with a sheet of virtual paper and a stylus clipped to a plastic tablet.

"The Independent Republic of Mars now operates like any bureaucracy, a pain we must endure. Sign on the bottom there."

Dale scribbled her name and handed the stylus to Ford, who added his signature.

▼

Outside, Dale turned toward her ex-husband. "Thank goodness that's settled. See you around the town, Brother Ford."

She moved to go, but Ford tugged at her sleeve.

"Hey, hey, hey, not so fast. Wait a damn Martian minute, will you?"

Dale stopped. She crossed her arms. "Why should I?"

Ford hesitated. He didn't want to make yet another mistake with this difficult woman. How to sustain the conversation?

"What's your favorite spot in the hab?" was the question he thought might work.

Dale tapped an impatient foot. "The Farm, of course. You've cooked up some dumb plan. What is it?"

Ford smiled at her predictable surliness. "Okay, here we go — I happen to know that Buster has set up a picnic for the two of us out there. Celebrate our freedom."

"You're kidding."

"You can't refuse, hurt Buster's feelings . . ."

Mayfield had spread a blanket under the apple trees, and on it placed salads, sandwiches, and pastries from the Barsoomian Bakery.

Dale grasped his arm to help lower herself with maidenly modesty. Ford tumbled down beside her.

"Here's a little something extra," said Mayfield, showing off a tall bottle and two plastic cups.

Ford raised a hand. "Whoa there, Buster. Business first."

He rose to one knee and held out the gold ring Dale had crafted for him. The diamond sparkled.

"Hesperia Dale," he said with carefully measured solemnity, *"will you marry me?"*

She scowled. "All this, the trees, the picnic, the damn ring I made, it's nothing but a plot to get on my good side."

Ford nodded. "True. Now answer the question."

Tears sprang into Dale's eyes. She shook her head to fend them off, took a breath to sort out her thoughts.

"All right, yes," she said at last. Her voice was shaking. "This time, okay, you got me. So I say . . . *yes."*

"Give me your hand."

Dale held out her left hand, and Ford slipped the ring on her fourth finger.

"There," he said.

Mayfield poured a brown liquid into two cups. "Technically, alcohol's no longer forbidden," said he. "And what do you know, Ed's got a thing going out in the repair bay. He sends his compliments."

Dale and Ford ceremoniously clicked plastic to plastic and drained their drinks.

50

A DOOR camouflaged to blend in with the Central Park walls rolled up at the touch of a hidden switch, and Motro, The Ark's all-purpose industrial robot, rolled out onto the simulated grass flooring.

Nilo Hoberman pressed a button on Motro's hand controller to stop him and tossed the device to Joe Ford.

"Now let's see what you can do."

Ford directed Motro out to the edge of the lake in stops and starts and brought him to a halt under the pipes and artificial clouds.

"What do you think? We there?"

Hoberman squinted up at the plumbing installation

"Turn in place ten degrees."

Ford tilted the joystick, and Motro pivoted around.

"That's better. Now open the stabilizers."

"How?" Ford shook the controller in frustration.

"Right shoulder button. Try it."

Ford ran his fingers over the controller and discovered a button behind the right hand grip. He squeezed, and four massive stabilizer arms extended outward from Motro's body.

The two men clambered aboard the work platform atop Motro's back. Hoberman pointed out a side button and joystick combination on the controller, and Ford raised the platform five stories in a slow and deliberate ascent.

"Do not rock boat," said Ford. He was starting to feel dizzy, and his slightest movement caused the work platform to sway alarmingly on its slender titanium pole.

"Okay, come up another foot or so."

Ford jockeyed the work platform upward, bringing it right underneath the bottom rung of a ladder.

"Make like a monkey, old man," said Hoberman. "and up we go. Easy peasy."

Ford watched Hoberman grab the ladder and haul himself into the park ceiling without ado. Whining piteously, Ford forced himself to follow.

Up among the pipes, a catwalk allowed free movement. Once Ford found his footing he began to breathe easier. But the plumbing elements all looked the same.

"Where is that damned gap?" he growled.

After three trips back and forth in the twisting and forking maze of pipes and spigots he found it.

"Hand me our replacement, Nilo."

Ford hefted the valve Dale printed up and screwed it into place. Hoberman attached the activating servo and wired it up.

"How do we test it?" he wondered.

Ford attached his multiprobe leads to the servo's electrical connections, one to each. He squeezed the handle. The servo rotated smartly, and the valve opened wide.

"But we're bone dry."

"Yeah, looks like there's more to the puzzle."

Hoberman started down the ladder.

"Hang on, Kiddo. Let's hear your story. Love's rocky road."

Hoberman glanced up at Ford. "You know all about that from a front row seat, I believe. For what it's worth, Thoo kissed me, and I didn't even ask."

"That's a start."

Back on the ground they hustled Motro back into his garage.

"Master valve? Where did they put it?" worried Ford.

"Over by the wading pool, I think," suggested his apprentice.

And sure enough, there Ford discovered a manhole cover disguised by a coating of fake grass. He pried it open. Exposed underneath was a large bronze valve. Putting forth all his strength he managed to turn the large red wheel on top.

"Whoa . . ."

They heard gurgling and banging as water forced its way across the park, up a wall, over the ceiling, and into the rain cloud above their heads, shaking the floor under their feet. But no rain fell.

Hoberman scratched his head. "Think this will ever work?"

Ford stared at the cloud. "Those pipes are old. They may crack under pressure, clog if rust inside gets loose. We don't dare test them to find out."

▼

PODCAST HOST:

Hello, out there. Thuvia, *The Real Maid of Mars,* coming at you from Central Park. While I'm talking, volunteers are hard at work decorating the place for today's big event. And now, before they tie the knot again, I corralled each of the betrothed — separately, of course, 'cause they're not supposed to see each other and jinx their union before the ceremony, right?

Here they are with a few words of, well, wisdom, I guess, huh? Hesperia? Bride again, what a journey.

DALE:

I'll say. I wasn't even hoping things would work out. Or, didn't know I was, if I was. The ups and downs, they were a test.

PODCAST HOST:

Hey, girl, you passed. Now let's hear from the groom. Joe? Got a honeymoon in mind?

FORD:

We're off to the Outpost. Take it easy, listen to the band, maybe dance a step or two. I hear the hydrogen plant has some problems, so I may have to make this a working holiday, be there for a while.

PODCAST HOST:

Safe travels, you two.

FORD:

Thanks, Thuvia. Now here's a question for *you*. Who's going to be a father to your son when he pops?

PODCAST HOST:

Ooh, that's a rude one. Zoran is on his way back to Earth, but it might work out with someone else.

FORD:

Work out with whom, may I ask?

PODCAST HOST:

You may not. (Pause.) But I'll tell you anyway. It looks like a nice young man we both know — no names today — may be signing up. Cross your fingers, wish us well.

DALE:

When this is over I'm going to toss you my artichoke blossom. Bouquet tradition, modified with a prickly thistle for Mars. That way, you're next.

▼

Later in the afternoon, Dale and Ford found themselves back in the park, wearing white wedding cassocks once again and once again surrounded by their fellow citizens.

Dale had tucked hibiscus flowers into her blonde hair. And, as advertised, she held a blooming artichoke thistle for her bouquet. Ford wore an origami rose Lofgren had fashioned from a paper copy of P.L. Scott's now famous political manifesto. Bride and groom were both strangely nervous, in spite of having done it all before.

Standing before them, Ismenius Pomerance read the proper litany from notes on his handheld.

"All right, Joseph . . . wilt thou have this woman to thy wedded wife, forsaking all others, till death do you part?"

"I will," said Ford.

The crowd murmured soft approval. No one was quite sure how to respond to the vows, eerily repeated from a prior ceremony.

"And thou, Hesperia, wilt thou have this man to thy husband,

and cleave unto him only, till death do you part?"

"I will," said she.

The crowd mumbled unintelligibly.

"Do thou, Joseph, promise to love and keep her, for better or for worse, till the end of your days?"

"I do."

"And do you, Hesperia, promise to love and keep him, in sickness and in health, till the end of your days?"

Dale swallowed and cleared her throat.

"I do."

"Is there a ring?" asked Pomerance.

"There is." Ford showed everyone the ring he rescued when Dale tore it off. She held out her hand, and he slipped it back onto her finger, now nestled up against her finely wrought diamond engagement ring.

"Hesperia?"

"Yes, there's another ring" — she lifted Ford's left hand above his head — "but he's already wearing it." She blushed. "You know, from before."

Ford leaned close and whispered into her ear. "Been there all the time."

Pomerance glanced around at the group. "Well, then, I think we've done it. On behalf of the Independent Republic of Mars, and in accordance with the laws that will hereafter rule over us, I now pronounce you man and wife."

Nilo Hoberman edged up behind Pomerance and pushed a small electronic device into his hand. Pomerance paused to examine it, noting a single green button on top. Hoberman pointed up at the ceiling. He wiggled his eyebrows.

"Ahh," said Pomerance, "the blessing. Joe, you may kiss the bride. And if God so chooses, *let it rain!*"

He pressed the green button.

Gurgling noises issued from the rain cloud. Pipes banged.

The crowd drew back.

"Not again," muttered Ford.

Then a torrent burst forth, a lashing downpour of biblical intensity.

"*That valve!*" exclaimed Dale. Ford nodded.

Some optimistic volunteer had made paper hats anticipating the traditional moment, and all at once everybody was wearing one.

Trivium Quinn opened an umbrella over President Pomerance. "Good job, sir," he said.

Joe Ford took Hesperia Dale in his arms.

The crowd, dampened in body but not in spirit, was now in a merry mood.

"Kiss her, Joe! Kiss your wife!" they chanted.

Bride and groom looked at each other.

"You ready?"

They were soaked to the skin in the pelting rain, and their kiss was a wet one.

▲ ▲ ▲

Afterword . . .

This story began long ago while I was toiling in Hollywood and first thought about writing a novel. The seeds were planted, but the fruit didn't ripen into a book because, after forty experimental pages, I veered into another career as a designer and developer of video games.

The original ideas stayed with me, however, and now, thirty-odd years later, they finally expanded into the tale you just read.

Made in the USA
Las Vegas, NV
12 December 2022

62173197R10174